S0-AEE-223

HER HEART & HIS CROWN

The Finale

3

A NOVEL BY

BIANCA

UF
Bianca

© 2017

Published by Royalty Publishing House
www.royaltypublishinghouse.com

ALL RIGHTS RESERVED

Any unauthorized reprint or use of the material is prohibited. No part of this book may be reproduced or transmitted in any form or by any means, electronic, or mechanical, including photocopying, recording, or by any information storage without express permission by the publisher.

This is an original work of fiction. Names, characters, places and incidents are either products of the author's imagination or are used fictitiously and any resemblance to actual persons, living or dead is entirely coincidental.

Contains explicit language & adult themes suitable for ages 16+

PILAR

*A*pproaching the door and seeing Detectives Sam Mcgrady and Cliff Jackson, I knew that it was about to be some shit. I didn't know that I was about to get arrested for the murder of Blizzy's ass.

"Ma'am, do you understand what you are being arrested for?" Sam asked me.

I nodded my head. After everything I'd been through, I didn't care what I was being arrested for.

"WHAT THE FUCK? SHE AIN'T..." Swan started.

I shushed her by putting my finger to her mouth. I ain't want them trying to bring her in. I know Swan will ride for me, but I don't know if she will ride for Duke. You know what? Fuck Duke.

"Let me slide on my shoes," I said to them.

I slid on my Nike slides and followed them out the door. They tried to handcuff me, but I wasn't going.

"Girl, we have to cuff you. You don't want me to throw you down and cuff you," Cliff spoke.

"Swan, can you record me telling them that I'm pregnant, so when they see how rough they are trying to handle me, I'll have all those jobs in my pocket," I said.

After I said that, they let me go, and I followed them out to the car.

"Pilar, I'm going to call Duke," Lee yelled out the door.

"NO!" I yelled back.

They put me in the backseat of the car and drove off. I would be scared if I did do this, but I know for a fact that I didn't do this. I mean, I know who pulled the trigger, but I ain't no damn snitch. The only problem I was having was figuring out who had me arrested for this shit. There were a couple of people on the list to choose from. Veronica. She was Blizzy's long time hoe, and plus we recently got into it at her job. She probably could have said something. Duke. I know he's pissed that he thinks I had an abortion, so he probably wanted to get back at me. I mean, but I didn't peg Duke to be that childish, but so be it. A couple of honorable mentions could be his stupid ass wife, Edwina, or his bad attitude ass brother, Bakari. They both could gain something by me going to jail, but fuck all of them.

When we pulled up to the station, there were several cameras outside ready to interview a bitch. I'm not cuffed, so whatever camera get in my face first, I'm knocking them the fuck out, and I mean that shit. I don't know why they did that shit to begin with. How would they feel if people bombarded them with cameras?

"Keep your head down, Pilar," Sam spoke.

I respected Sam because Sam was the nice one, and he just seemed like he wanted to do his job, but that Cliff was a stupid ass dick. Sam must've not known who the fuck I was because I ain't putting my head down for no-fucking-body. As soon as I stepped out the car, they were trying to duck my head, but I moved their hands. I was bombarded with questions, and even more ridiculous statements.

"Pilar, over here, was Brandon cheating on you?" one reporter asked.

"Pilar, over here, did you think you would never be caught?" another reporter asked.

"Pilar, over here, how could you do such a ruthless thing? Why didn't you just break up with him?" the next reporter asked, before I lost it.

Using all my might, I pushed the lens of her big ass camera, and she stumbled back and fell.

Staring her directly into her eyes, I replied, "How was that for ruthless? Don't fuck with me, bitch. Keep that damn camera out of my face!"

Cliff yoked me up and dragged me through the doors. If I hadn't been able to walk fast, he would have been dragging me on my knees. As I was keeping up with him, something…no, someone caught my eye. I saw Demarkus. He was in an office, talking to an older man. He saw me and did a double take. I was being dragged so fast that I didn't have time to read the name on the door. We finally made it to a room at the end of the hall. I was thrown into a very cold room, into a very cold steel chair, with nothing on my arms or legs. As soon as my skin touched the cold steel, chill bumps appeared all over my body. They both took a seat and stared at me like I was about to start talking first.

"So, do you know why we brought you here, Ms. Harrison?" Sam asked politely.

"Well, when you showed up at my door, you said that I was under arrest for the murder of Brandon Lewis," I replied.

"Cut the smart shit. We know you know who did it," Cliff spat.

I rolled my eyes at him.

"Well, Mr. Cliff..."

"Detective."

"*Detective* Cliff, according to you and your partner, the reason you stepped foot on my doorstep is because I was arrested for the murder of Brandon Lewis. Now, which one is it? Do you think I know who did it? Or did I do it? I am confused," I said, waving my hands in circular motions next to my head.

BOOM!

Cliff slammed his hands on the table like that was supposed to scare me. I didn't even jump, but I chuckled at him.

"Um, Pilar, would you like some water?" Sam asked.

"No, Detective Sam, I am fine. Your partner is becoming unhinged. It looks like he needs the water more than me," I said and nodded my head at him.

"If you weren't a woman, I swear⊠" he started.

"You swear what? You'd practice police brutality?" I cut him off.

He was getting pissed off, and I was loving it. He couldn't be more pissed off than I already was, so what the fuck ever.

"Take a break, Cliff," Sam spoke.

"I'm good," he replied.

"Look, Ms. Harrison, I am sorry for my partner's reaction, but he is just upset. He doesn't want this case to go cold. We want to bring his family some justice, and we feel like you can help with that. Will you help us, or⬚" Sam was cut off by Cliff.

"⬚Or would you like to go to prison for something you didn't do? Your kid will be born in jail, and you will never see it grow up."

"Didn't he tell you to take a break?" I asked Cliff.

"Look, whoever told you that I know something about this lied. Maybe you should have asked that person who told you that I knew something. Nine times out of ten, the person that called to give the information be the person that knows the most. I would like a phone call now. Do I get one of those?"

"Sure," Sam said. "Well, after you assaulted the camera lady outside, I have to cuff you."

"First of all, she assaulted me. You didn't see her with that damn camera in my face. Had she stayed back like the rest of the mothafuckas, I wouldn't have pushed her on her shit. Just do what you gotta do, and take me to the damn phone," I spat and held my hands out.

"Pilar, you do know that you are too beautiful of a woman to talk the way that you talk. No man is going to want a woman that talk as nasty as you," Sam spoke softly. "It's really not attractive."

"Well, have you ever thought that I talk the way I talk for myself and not for others. If *you* don't think the way I talk is attractive, then maybe I'm not trying to attract *you*. Anything else?" I spoke, and rolled my eyes.

Sam smirked at what I said and then guided me to a phone. The phone wasn't really isolated like I hoped it would be, but it was good enough. This phone was at a desk that overlooked the other desks. If I talked loud enough, people could hear me. I can't believe that I am going to waste my phone call on this fool, but a part of me felt like this was him. I don't think that Veronica is smart enough to do some shit like this, especially after I have whooped her ass before. This had Duke written all over it…or did it?

"Do you know the phone number?" Sam asked as we took a seat by the phone.

I sucked my teeth and rolled my eyes at him because he just asked a stupid ass question. I'm sure he could tell how annoyed I was just by the way that I was looking at him.

Of course, I know the fucking number. That was a stupid ass question. I thought to myself.

"Yes, I know the number. Can I get just a little privacy, please? Just a little?" I pleaded.

"I can't give you much privacy, but I'll step a couple feet away from you," he said and stepped away.

I did the best I could at picking the phone up with the cuffs on. I dialed that stupid ass nigga's number. It was a good thing that I didn't have to call collect because he would have declined my damn phone call; that I am sure of. The phone rang two times before he answered.

"Duke," his sexy deep accented voice said into the phone.

His voice is…fucking…ah…fuck. *Get it together, Pilar.*

"Duke," he said again.

"You are in-fucking-credible. I don't give a damn about you not believing me about your sick ass father, but for you to have me arrested, Duke, is a new fucking low, even for you. What was the..."

"Pilar, what the..."

"Shut the fuck up. What was the fucking reason behind this shit? I have never done anything to you besides love your stupid black ass, and the way that..."

"Pilar..."

"Shut...the...fuck...up. The way that you did me. First, you LIE about having a bitch. Now you got a wife, and a baby on the way. Second, you get mad at me, for wanting to get rid of something, that I *thought* didn't belong to you, and THEN when I tell you the reason, you wig out on me, like your fucking father is incapable of being a fucking piece of shit. Duke, I swear..."

"Will you shut..."

"No, and I swear to God, if I wasn't done with your ass before, I am done with your ass now. If I wasn't⊠"

"PILAR..."

"...a solid ass bitch, the real fucking murderer would be in jail right now. As bad as that mothafucka should be in jail, I'm⊠"

Dial tone!

I know this mothafucka didn't hang up on me, I thought to myself. I was getting ready to call him back when I looked up and saw Cliff holding the plug in his hand. I took a deep breath because I wanted to curse that mothafucka out.

"Time's UP!" he smirked.

Sam picked me up out the chair and was leading me back to the cold room. When I stepped back in the room, Demarkus was now in there, along with the old man whose office he was in when I first saw him. Demarkus was looking fine as hell. Jesus fucking Christ. He had a creased button down white shirt, paired with some blue Chino's, a brown pair of pants, and brown belt. He had his gun and badge on his side, and I instantly felt my pussy getting wet. You could see his muscles through his shirt, and I swear I just wanted to fuck him. He's fine, got good dick, and he paid. That is the perfect trio, but that nigga married, and I instantly got turned off when I saw that ring on his hand. I rolled my eyes at him and sat down in the cold seat.

"Captain Green," Cliff and Sam greeted him in unison.

"Demarkus," Cliff sneered.

"Ugh! I thought you were just a dick to women. You're a dick to men too. Do better. The jealousy is seeping through your veins, and my friend, it's not a good look," I said to him and rolled my eyes.

"Gentlemen, give me a few moments alone with Ms. Harrison, please," he spoke, and they left out of the room. "Gooley, you stay."

Once they closed the door, there was a very awkward silence in the room. It's like I could feel the tension thickening in this damn room. I wondered if these fools thought that they could make me say something about that damn killing.

"Pilar, how are you?" the guy I knew as Captain Green spoke.

"About as great as I'm going to be, considering the fact that I am handcuffed in a police station, yourself?" I asked.

"Um. I don't know how to tell you this, but…I am your umm, grandfather."

I chuckled to myself and then threw my head back into a hearty laugh. This has really got to be fuck with Pilar Harrison day.

"It's true, P. You remember when I told you back at the…yeah. He's your grandfather."

I had completely forgotten about that conversation that took place at the hotel.

"Oh, at the hotel, right before we fucked, you told me about *my grandfather*," I said and winked at him.

Captain Green grimaced at my words and then turned to glare at Demarkus. His face was turning red. I don't know if it was from embarrassment or anger, but it wasn't my problem. He turned and looked back at me.

"Um, I know that this may have come off as a shock to you, but it's true. Cisco, your mother, was my daughter," he said and tried to grab my cuffed hands that were on the table, but I moved them and stared at him with a death stare, letting him know not to try to touch me again.

"This pertains to this case, how?" I asked, changing the subject.

I was not trying to get into this conversation with this man about being my grandfather. We don't need to talk about this because I don't want to hear any sorry excuse that he may come up with for the reason he just now making contact. As far back as I can remember, I don't remember him being in my life. So as far as I'm concerned, he can keep his fucking introduction. The same goes for Prince Harrison. I don't know what type of 'Come to Jesus' meeting he had to make him want to suddenly be in my life, but that was just a waste of a meeting that Jesus could have had with someone else. I have only had two consistent people in my life. That was Swan and my deceased ass grandma, and that's how I plan to keep it.

"It doesn't, but I thought that☒" he started.

"Well, you thought wrong."

"Pilar, I know that this may☒"

He tried to grab my cuffed hands again, but I guess he thought about the look that he just got from me.

"Look, Captain Green, I honestly don't know if you think I'm joking or not. I don't know if my facial expression is giving off something that my mouth is not saying, but I honestly don't want to hear anything about you being my grandfather again. I'm laughing, but I am dead ass serious. So, call Detective Dick and Sam back in here, so we can continue this show," I spoke.

The room got silent again. Demarkus and Captain Green were staring at me just like I was staring back at them.

"So, they got you here on murder☒" Captain Green started.

"No, they got me here thinking that I know the person who murdered Brandon. I haven't murdered anyone," I cut him off.

"Pilar, you know I can't help you if you don't tell me the truth."

"Yeah, yeah, yeah, those other guys told me that too. So, it looks like I'm about to have a long seventy-two hours in front of me. That is the longest that they can hold me, right? If y'all had evidence, I would be charged."

BOOM!

Slamming his fist against the table, Captain Green yelled, "DAMN IT, PILAR!"

"Is that a tactic that all you police people use? The banging on the table is really not scary. You guys should change that." I chuckled. "You're not the only one that's frustrated, Captain Green. Believe me."

We stared at each other momentarily. In that moment, I took in his features. Cisco was definitely a spitting image of him. The cheekbones, the eyes, and the funny shaped nose. If I wasn't a spitting image of my sperm donor, I would try to look for any features that I may have gotten from him. He was an alright looking man, who probably slept with Lenora as a one night stand. Now that I think about it, he couldn't have been a one-night stand because he actually knew about Cisco. He knew about me. He shrugged his shoulders, left out the room, and then Demarkus took a seat in his chair.

"Pilar, you know you don't have to be mean to him," Demarkus said, breaking the silence.

"You won't tell me who I will and won't be mean to. He is a coward, and I don't deal with those kinds of people. Escort me to my cell, or leave me alone. I don't feel like talking to people—you included. You're excused."

I put my head on my cuffed hands and closed my eyes. Moments later, I heard the door open and close. I knew that this was about to be a long seventy-two hours, but this was a cake-walk compared to what I've been through.

DUKE

I was laying across the bed when Pilar's phone call came through. That little mothafucka wouldn't let me get a word in edgewise. Like, I could not get a word in at all. I was so pissed. I wondered what the fuck that was about. I grabbed my computer and Googled a news outlet in Florida. As soon as I pulled it up, I saw the headline that pissed me off.

Pilar Harrison, Suspected Murderer of Brandon Lewis.

They also played a video of Pilar pushing the newswoman down. I chuckled to myself because that was how Pilar was. If you got in her face, then she was not going to back down. She doesn't care who you are, and that is one of the things that I loved about her. The whole conversation played through my head. I tried to break down some of the shit she said. It was a good thing that I recorded this phone call. I recorded it because I was sick about this girl, and I loved hearing her voice, even if she was cursing me the fuck out. I was fucking obsessed with this girl.

I don't care if you don't believe me about your sick ass father…

This was the second time that she'd said that, and I had to get to the bottom of this. Man, what the fuck do people expect me to believe?

Man, this shit put me in between a rock and a hard place. Listen, how the fuck would you feel if the person you love told you that the person that raised you for the better part of your life raped them? Listen, I was not dismissing what Pilar said totally, but why didn't she tell me this from the beginning? My dad had never had problems getting a woman. Hell, he had four wives. What was so special that he wanted to rape Pilar? Am I being stupid? Am I being naïve? Is my dad blinding me? If he did do that shit, how the fuck would I get Pilar to forgive me for not believing her? What the fuck would I do to him for fucking with my girl and potentially ruining the best thing that ever happened to me?

Getting me arrested is a new low, even for you...

First, I would never get her arrested. As pissed off as I am at her for aborting my fucking child, I would never have her arrested. Pilar is my whole fucking world. I mean, after she aborted my baby, I can admit that I truly overreacted, and should have never ever put my hands on her, but you got to look at where I'm coming from. I'm so in love with this girl, and for her to get rid of my child because of some other shit I got going on, was selfish as fuck. Money was not going to be an issue with caring for my child. Ahh, just thinking about what she went through to get that shit scooped out of her, pissed me off. What if she never gets a chance to have another baby?

See, the next part of the phone call was where it got tricky. Pilar's verbiage. was something. She can tell you one thing and really mean another, but you can't call her a liar because she did tell you...just not how you expected her to.

First, you LIE about having a bitch. Now you got a wife, and a baby on the way. Second, you get mad at me for wanting to get rid of something that I thought didn't belong to you, and THEN when I tell you the reason, you wig out on me like your fucking father is incapable of being a fucking piece of shit.

I had to listen to this part a few times because all I heard in this part of the phone call is "Duke, I'm still pregnant, and I thought the baby didn't belong to you." That was all I heard. I was getting ready to play the next part, when I heard the door open and close. I knew that it was Edwina, and I instantly got an attitude. See, something she said at the wedding has been on mind, and this phone call just made her look even more suspect.

"Hey, Prince, what are you doing?" she asked.

"What does it look like I am doing, Edwina," I snapped.

"Well, the nursery is almost complete, and this little baby will be here in a couple of weeks. Aren't you excited?" she said, and laid on her back next to me, while I laid on my stomach still searching the internet.

"Sure," I replied.

"Duke, what is the problem? I'm staying out of your way like you asked me to do, but I would think that you would like to be updated on your child."

"Edwina, I'm going to ask you a question, and you better be fucking honest with me, and if you're not, that baby is not going to stop me from beating your fucking ass," I snapped.

"What, Duke? I ain't never had a reason to lie to you, so I'm not going to start now."

"Back at our wedding, you said that you were going to stay away from me, and you made sure that Pilar was going to stay away from me as well, or something along the lines of that. What did you mean by that?"

"I don't remember saying that," she simply lied.

"Alright, Edwina. Same question, different answer, and last time to tell me the truth."

"Alright, damn! I called the tip hotline on her, sue me. Our relationship was good until she came around. Now that she is in jail, we can work on us."

I was getting ready to respond to what she said when it fully registered in my head what she said.

"Edwina, how did you know about Brandon? How did you know to call the tip hotline and tell them that it was Pilar who did that?"

"I didn't *say* she did it. I said she might know who did it. I just did it to scare her, and so she would leave you alone. I want our old life back."

"You didn't answer neither question that I asked you," I spoke through gritted teeth while glaring at her.

"I may have heard..."

"EDWINA, DON'T FUCKIN' PLAY WITH ME," I barked at her.

"Bakari and I were talking, and he let it slip, and...."

"You and Bakari were talking?"

She nodded her head slowly.

"And he let it slip?"

She nodded her head again. I got out the bed and slid on my shoes.

"Duke, please don't..." she started before she tried to get off the bed.

"Edwina, shut the fuck up. Don't tell me what the fuck to do. Bakari had no right to open his fucking mouth, and you...don't get even get me started on your stupid ass!"

I walked out the door with Edwina right on my heels. Taking the stairs two at a time, Baron was coming up two at a time.

"I gotta holla at you, bro," Baron said.

"I already know. I'm going to go handle part of the situation now," I replied.

"BARON, YOU HAVE TO STOP HIM! HE'S GOING TO KILL BAKARI," Edwina yelled from behind me.

"Duke," Baron called my name. "What the fuck is going on?" Baron caught up to me, but I ignored him.

I was on a mission to find that nigga who thought it was okay to tell this bitch our business. This nigga forgot all about bro code, and I would be surprised if he ain't tried to fuck her. The way she is acting about Pilar, her ass probably already fucked him just to think she on some getting back at me type shit. I was looking all over the house for that nigga, but he was nowhere to be found. Walking out back, I saw him, Bomani, Mariah, my mothers, my father, grandparents, and a couple of more guys sitting at a table along with a camera crew. I couldn't quite place the other guys, but I was quite sure it had something to do with the meeting that was placed on my calendar for today that I was not going to be in attendance for. Not caring about looking stupid or ruining my family's reputation, I was damn near skipping to the table. My adrenaline was running rampant through my veins, so I had to get to this nigga before I had a heart attack.

"BAKARI, RUNNN!" Edwina shrieked from behind me.

Bakari looked but didn't have time to move out of his seat.

"Son, we were waiting..." my dad started.

BAM!

I cut my dad off and connected with Bakari's jaw. He tried to stand up, but I latched on to the back of his neck.

BAM! BAM! BAM!

I slammed his head into his plate three times. I was trying to drown that nigga in ranch dressing. He ate too much of the shit anyway. Baron tried to grab me to no avail. My whole fucking family knew to let me calm the fuck down on my own when I was pissed. I didn't know where my strength came from because I was so much stronger than my brothers.

"You running your fucking mouth to Edwina," I growled in his ear.

BAM! I didn't even give him a chance to answer before I slammed his now bloody face into the cracked plate. *BAM!*

"Dukkkee," Bakari groaned, spitting out blood and ranch at the same time.

I could hear the screams, and I could feel people tugging on my body. The more they tugged, the harder I latched on to his neck.

I ignored their pleas. The only thing on my mind was murking my fucking brother.

"My girl in jail because of that shit!"

BAM!

"She so solid that she ain't even ratted on yo' bitch ass, nigga."

BAM! BAM! BAM!

I slammed his head three more times until his body went limp. I was going to slam his head one more time before I felt someone latch onto my neck. It brought me down to my knees. I was getting ready to start swinging, but it was my grandpa. That nigga was strong. Old or not, he would beat your ass and not apologize for it.

"Take your black ass in the house and calm the fuck down. I hope you ain't killed your damn brother on live TV," my grandpa hissed into my ear.

I got off my knees, dusted myself off, and walked back toward the house. Edwina and my daddy weren't around. Edwina was next. I didn't know what I was going to do to her, but she was definitely going to get some of this wrath too.

"Bomani…Baron, go follow your brother and make sure he don't harm his wife," my grandpa ordered them. I cringed at the word *wife*.

I didn't even look back, but I could hear them screaming about the ambulance. I walked in the house and started searching for Edwina. I could hear Bomani and Baron's feet behind me.

"Duke, wait up for a minute," Baron spoke.

I was not trying to hear anything that he was saying. It was already on my mind to choke that bitch out when I got to her. Bakari and she were probably plotting on Pilar since neither one of them liked her. Bakari didn't even have a reason not to like Pilar. He was just being an asshole. I expected this shit from Edwina because she had a reason to be pissed. Hell, I cheated on her and fell in love with the other woman.

By the time I made it to the hall where my dad's office was, they were both coming out, and she stared at me with tears in her eyes.

"Duke, my water broke," she whispered.

My anger instantly went away as I went to help her.

PILAR

*S*ee, I was supposed to get out of jail after seventy-two hours, but they claimed that bitch pressed charges for pushing her ugly ass down. They were hating and wouldn't even let Swan post bail for me. They were trying to get me to rat out Bakari's ass, but that was a no. Telling on Bakari would be like telling on Duke since the hit came directly from Duke. As much as I hated him, I didn't want to rat him out. Trust me, I'm sure after that phone call, Duke probably beat his ass. If Duke was still the same Duke that I met and had grown to love, yeah, he beat his ass.

Sleeping on this fucking cot for the last couple of days really had my back and side fucked up. It was safe to say that jail was not for me at all. I was supposed to be getting out of here tomorrow, but we would see how that went. I was ready to eat some real damn food, because I swear to God that this food was something that they would feed pigs on those farms in Mississippi. If my kids were anything like me, this food was going to come back up. The only thing that I was trying to keep down was some water. I knew people could survive on water for a long time. I had just grabbed my water bottle when the officer called my name.

"Harrison, you got a visitor."

I grabbed my water bottle and followed him. I knew it wasn't Swan or Lee because they should've been at work. I was put back into a cold room with a man in a suit. He was an older man with a salt and pepper beard. He looked very sophisticated in his tailored suit.

"Good afternoon, Ms. Harrison. My name is Preston Lane, and I am going to be your lawyer."

"Hi, Preston Lane. I'm sorry, but why do I need a lawyer? I didn't do anything," I spoke.

"I know, and that is why I'm here. Duke sent me here just in case..."

"Okay, you can go. Seriously. I don't need anything from Duke, or you. I'm getting out of here tomorrow. Thank you, but no thanks," I said, and got up from the table.

"He said that you would say that, but I'm going to give you my card. You can call me whenever you need me."

He held the card in his hand, but I stared at it and didn't take it. After he saw that I wasn't going to take it, he slid the card in the pocket of the hideous jumpsuit I was wearing. I couldn't wait to get out of here because I was going to shower and scrub my skin hard. Preston got up, knocked on the door, and they let him out of the room. The guard told me to get back in my seat because I had another visitor. A few moments later, this short thick ass woman walked in the room. She had on a pencil skirt, a tailored button down, and a blazer.

"Hey, Pilar. You are even more beautiful than you were described to me. My name is Serena Taylor. Your father, Prince Harrison, asked me to come here to take care of your case."

Squinting my eyes at her, I replied, "Look, you really wasted your time coming here. I don't have a case, and I really don't want any help from the likes of Prince Harrison."

I don't know what's up with the sorry ass men in my life, but this sending a lawyer shit was not going to make up for the shit storm they caused in my life.

"Your dad and I are good friends, and he wants you out of jail," Serena spoke.

"That's cool and all, but I'm good. Listen, I want to get back to my cell so I can get some rest."

She rolled her eyes and left out of the room. I tried to leave again, but the guard told me to sit down again. If it was another lawyer, I was going to scream. I was staring at the wall, and another young man came in the room. He didn't look like he could be a lawyer, but we would see what happened.

"What's up, Pilar? My name is Ryder Sanford, Jr. My father is Robert's best friend, and he wanted me to work on your case," he spoke smoothly. He stood there with his hand stretched out, waiting for me to shake it, but I couldn't. I just wanted to stare at him.

This man was a work of art. He looked like he was the same age as me or a few years older. He was tall and chocolate just the way that I liked them. He wasn't dressed like the other lawyers. The way he was dressed immediately attracted me to him. He had on a plain white t-shirt, a pair of Levi's that hung at his waist, and a pair of Jordans. I was not really into tennis shoes, but these were nice as fuck.

"How are you a lawyer? You look the same age as me," I finally replied. "You don't dress like a lawyer. The other lawyers that came in here had on suits, and here you are in jeans and a t-shirt."

"Well, Ms. Harrison, I save the suits for the courtroom. When I'm not in court, this is what I dress like. I actually saw you on TV pushing that stupid reporter down, and my dad said that Mr. Robert called him, but my dad sent me. Between you and me, I'm happy you pushed that woman down. She so pushy, and think she can't be touched," he said and laughed.

Even his laugh was sexy, and he had straight teeth.

"Okay, you keep saying, Robert? Who is that?"

"Captain Green, your grandfather."

I blew out a sigh of frustration because I didn't know why Robert thought I would take any help from him. He was out of his mind.

"Um, Ryder, listen. I don't need his help nor do I want it. You are so fine that I just don't want to let you leave just yet. So, tell me something about yourself."

"That's really nice of you, Pilar. Um, I never really know what to say when people say tell me about yourself. I'm twenty-seven with no kids, and I live in my own house" He chuckled. "Honestly, that's usually what women want to know when they want to know about a man. They don't ever want to know if you got a girlfriend or wife, which I don't, but you get what I'm saying."

"Honestly, I do like to know. My stupid ass baby daddy lied about his wife, and I don't know if she had the baby or not. Hell, he is about to run a whole damn country. He lied about that. I don't even know why he lied, to be honest. It's not like I wanted him for his money. It's ridiculous. I still don't, even though I know he's worth millions. I have the keys to his house and cars, but that shit doesn't impress me. I didn't have that shit when I was growing up."

"You're pregnant?" he asked.

I nodded my head before replying, "I went to get an abortion, but... never mind."

I cut the conversation off because I realized that I would have to tell him about the rape, and I didn't want to talk about that anymore with anyone. He reached across the table and grabbed my hands.

"You can talk about it whenever you want. I'll always have a listening ear. Well, I got to get back to the office, and you gotta get back to the...you know. I'm going to give you my card. My personal number is on the back if you want to give me a call when you get out," he said while handing me his card.

We both got up from the table at the same time. I couldn't hug him because I was cuffed, but he wrapped his arms around me, and his cologne smelled so good. He pulled away and knocked on the door so the guard could let him out. I guess I was done with visitors for today because he led me back to my cell since visiting time was over. I never thought I'd see the day that I'd be locked up. At least I didn't have a fucking cell mate.

"Pilar, you only got eight more hours. Just eight. You can make it, girl," I whispered to myself as I stared at the ceiling.

I was so ready to be in my own bed. As soon as I closed my eyes, I heard keys jingling in the cell door. My eyes popped back open, but I didn't budge.

"Pilar? It's me, your grandfather. Are you asleep?"

I didn't say anything at all. I just hoped he would go away. There was nothing that he could want me with me.

"Pilar, I know you are not sleeping. Listen. Your grandmother and I, God rest her soul, had a one-night thing. It only happened one time. It was one of the best nights of my life, to be honest. We were both drunk and high. I promise you, she never told me that she was pregnant. I didn't know about Cisco until she was five years old. Um, I knew she was mine the moment I laid eyes on her. She really was the spitting image of me. I couldn't say anything because…my wife was there. My wife is Lenita… Lenora's twin sister. That's why the situation was so complicated. I never had any more kids. I think that was God's way of punishing me for not doing what I was supposed to do for Cisco. My wife always wanted kids, but she could never get pregnant. Pilar, I know I was a piece of shit, and I could have done better by Cisco, but I want to do it right with you," he spoke lowly.

The tears were slowly sliding down the sides of my face. My face was so hot, and I didn't want to sniff because I didn't want him to know that I was awake. What type of piece of shit fucks a pair of twin sisters, gets one pregnant, and slides out of her life? Well, at least I know where my twins came from. I had to know. He was getting ready to leave, but I shot off several questions. I had to know.

"Lenita never questioned the looks of Cisco since she looks just like you? What happened at the reunion? Why did you never tell your wife?" I whispered.

"Well, that reunion was the last time your great aunt, and

grandmother spoke to each other. I don't know why they stopped talking, and she never told me. Maybe she put two and two together. If she did, she never mentioned it to me. At the reunion, I pulled Lenora aside and told her that she was wrong for keeping her pregnancy away from me."

"I'm sure that if my grandma had told you about her pregnancy, you probably would have made her get rid of it. You never told your wife because you were a coward, and I'm sure that she is just as uppity as my sperm donor's family. You were wrong, and now you are feeling remorseful, and I really don't know why. My mom has been dead for ten years, and Lenora's been gone for several years. I'm damn near twenty-five years old. We really ain't got shit to catch up on, to be honest. I don't want to look in the face of my grandmother's twin, especially if they are identical. It'll be too much. Just go," I whispered. "GO!" I yelled at him after I saw that he was not moving as fast as I would have liked.

When he slipped out the cell, I held the pillow up to my face and cried myself to sleep.

∞

I wish that it was easier to just walk out of jail when you were free, but the processing out took longer than it did to book me. I was just ready to get home, shower, and eat. While I was sitting there waiting, Robert came out of his office and asked me to step inside. I had time to spare, so I went into his office.

"Happy to be going home?" he asked.

I'm sure he knew that was a dumb question. Of course, I was happy to be going home. I guess that was one of those ice breaker questions. While he was talking, I took a gander at his office. There were pictures of him everywhere, and then I stopped on one picture of him and his wife. There was barely any food in my stomach, but what was left came up. I fell to my knees at the garbage can and threw up. Robert held my hair while I dry heaved in the garbage can.

"Here you go," he said, handing me a bottle of water off his desk.

I took a sip of the water. Robert helped me to my feet, and there was another picture of them on his desk. I tapped my stomach hoping that it would settle down. They looked so much alike, and it was sickening. It was really like looking at my grandmother.

"Was sleeping with my grandma a mistake? I mean, they are identical. Like…did you think that she was your wife or something?" I asked.

"No. I knew it was Lenora. Not that it helps any now, but I always felt like I got with the wrong sister. Lenita was…is something that I'm not nor will I ever be.Back in the day, before she had Cisco, she was fun! Lenita was…you know… one of those types of women who felt like the wind that blew owed her something. The only thing about Lenora was the fact that she didn't know how, as you young people say, to turn down. That was her only problem."

"Wow! I really don't know what to say to that," I whispered.

"Can I ask you a question? You don't have to answer it if you don't want."

"Sure."

"Are you having a baby?"

I nodded my head, but I didn't want to go into detail.

"Do you want to go out for dinner? I'm not saying today, tomorrow, or next week, but soon. I want to get to know you, Pilar. I'm going to give you my number, and I want you to call me so we can talk."

I offered him a weak smile and took his number. The lady that was processing me out told me that I was done and free to leave whenever.

"You need a ride home?" he asked.

"No, my friend should be out here waiting for me."

I walked out his office and walked out the damn jail. The sun on my skin felt amazing. I looked around and expected to see black trucks lined up outside, but I didn't, which was kind of upsetting. I didn't even see Swan's ass, so I sat on the curb. I was only sitting on the curb for two minutes before Swan swerved into the parking lot on two wheels.

"Come on, bittccchhh!" Swan yelled over the loud music.

I hopped in her car, and she had food. I instantly went for the damn food.

"Girl, I had been waiting out here for a couple of hours, but I didn't hear from you, so I dipped to get some food. I knew you would be hungry since your little ass told me you hadn't been eating. You ain't been feeding my godchildren? So, what were they asking you? You didn't get finger banged, did you?"

I shook my head and laughed at her as I stuffed the food down my throat. Swan was going to always be Swan, and there was nothing I could change about that. I took a few more bites before I decided to explain everything that happened in just a week of being in jail.

She listened intently as I told her about those two detectives trying to get me to rat on Bakari's bitch ass. I told her about meeting my grandfather and how I didn't know if I wanted to give him a chance or not. I told her about the three lawyers that each of the stupid men in my life tried to send for me. I wanted to keep Ryder a secret, but I couldn't. I couldn't wait to call him whenever I got shit situated in my life.

"So, my little jailbird, do you want to go out tonight?" Swan asked. "We gotta celebrate you getting out of jail."

"Girl, shut the fuck up. I was only in jail a week. You acting like I was gone for three years or something."

We pulled into our yard, and I damn near ran full speed in the house. I ran me a hot bubble bath, dropped two big bath bombs in the hot water, and watched the water turn shades of blue and red. They were going to get all this dirt and grime off my skin. My phone was charging while the water was cooling off, so I decided to step back into the living room to talk to Swan.

"So, have you heard from Baron?" I asked Swan as she was sitting in front of the TV.

"I talk to Baron every day. Ask what you want to ask, Pilar."

"Um…has he said anything about… me and Duke."

"Well, Duke killed his brother on live TV! I'm kidding, but I'm sure Bakari would much rather be dead. It's all over social media. You better look it up."

I turned to walk away, and then she said something else that made me want to cry.

"Oh, and Edwina had the baby," she yelled out.

I really could have done without that information, but whatever. I hoped whatever they had was very healthy since they were waiting for the birth to figure out what they were having. I walked into the bathroom, grabbed my phone off the charger, and stepped in the tub. As soon as I got comfortable in the tub, it was like I could feel the dirt and grime melting off my body. I had to get on social media to see what this video was that Swan was talking about. When I powered my phone on, tons of messages came through to my phone. It damn near froze my phone up. I put my phone on the side of the tub and waited for the phone to stop beeping so I could go through them.

Duke: Pilar, I recorded our phone call, and I listened to it over and over again. I must ask. Are you still pregnant? Did you not have the abortion?

Duke: Pilar, if you didn't have the abortion, I'm sorry for not hearing you out. If you did, I'm not sorry for smacking the fuck out of you.

Duke: Pilar, you really got me fucked up, man. I can't even think straight. What you do to me?

Duke: I wanted a family with you.

Duke: I love you! I know you won't see these until you get out, but I love you, Pilar. I swear I do. I'm sending over a lawyer for you. Hope he helps.

Baron: Who you think you are, fighting on camera? You are funny. Stay up! Duke is a fucking mess without you, sis. Let me be the first to let you know, that I ain't never dismissed your claims about our father.

Fredrick: Shorty, hit me up when you get out.

31

Baron: Sis, I don't know if this will help you, but Duke reacted the way that he did because all his life he has tried to do shit to make our father happy. Our father is like a God to Duke, and think that nigga can do no wrong. The only time he got buck with our dad was when he was talking shit about you, believe or not. He ain't recently start to actually live life until you came into his life. I ain't telling you this because I'm his brother, I'm telling you this because it's the truth. That nigga was fucked up behind that shit, and the night of the wedding, that nigga cried out for you, in his damn sleep. LOL! I know you don't want to relive that night over again, so I'mma keep talking to Duke my damn self. I'mma send you this video of him crying. This is also the longest text messages I have ever sent in life. You better be glad I love you. 1 video attached*

I could honestly believe what Baron was saying about Duke and his unhealthy ass attachment to his dad. When we first got together, Duke was scared to do anything because he didn't want to displease his dad. I mean, everything I tried to get him to do, he would worry about if reporters saw us or it getting back to his dad. It was ridiculous, but it was all good.

I pulled up my social media, put Duke's name in the search bar, and a ton of videos pulled up. There were so many videos that it took forever to find where it originated. Duke was banging his head against that plate until it broke. I don't know what Duke was saying to him because he was whispering in his ear, but I know it had to be something that he didn't want the world to hear. The nosey side of me wanted to text him and see what happened, but the 'Fuck Duke' part of me left it alone.

I turned some music on and placed the phone on the side of the tub. I leaned my head back against the tub and continued to rub my belly. I was going to get through this… one way or the other.

DUKE

$\mathcal{G}$one.

Pilar had me gone. That girl got me so fucked up to the point where I damn near killed my brother on live TV. He had to get a lot of stitches in his face. I gave him a concussion, and he was knocked out for a couple of hours. I was embarrassed for my family. The shame I brought upon my family literally made me sick to my stomach. The only high part in my life right now was the fact that Edwina pushed out a healthy baby girl a few days ago. I also felt like an ass because I was the reason she went into labor early. Well, it wasn't too early because she was going to get induced next week anyway, but you get the point. I let my anger get the best of me, but I still had so many questions. Why were she and Bakari talking about Brandon? Instead of handling shit the way I did, I should have just put them both in the room at the same time, so neither one of them could lie. They would have had to tell the truth.

Brielle Ramses.

That's my daughter's name. It means 'God is my strength.' I was hoping that we would have a boy, but I was happy that she was healthy. I was holding her in my arms while I rocked in the rocking chair. No one had been by to see her except Baron, Bomani, and my grandfather. The rest of my family has been at Bakari's side, basically treating me like I was the black sheep, but I ain't give a fuck. He shouldn't have been running his mouth.

Edwina, the baby, and I were supposed to have been going home today, but she had an infection. One of them nasty ass nurses came in and didn't wash her hands. I'm glad that she didn't touch the baby. Edwina was heavily medicated, and I watched her while she slept. She was sleeping on her side, facing me. I couldn't deny that she was very beautiful, but something was off with her. I looked down at Brielle, and I just didn't feel right. I thought that the more that I held her, the more this feeling would go away. It was a feeling that a father was not supposed to have for his child. I didn't have a connection with her. I knew she was not even a week old yet, but she was not tugging at my heart strings like I thought that she would. She was beautiful and the spitting image of her mother. She had smooth light skin and when she opened her eyes, they were the same shade of hazel as her mother's. I always thought that the Ramses had strong genes, but I guess she did too.

Knock! Knock!

I got up and opened the door, and it was my grandfather. I walked back over to the rocking chair and sat down.

"Grandpa, I know you must be so ashamed of me. I'm sorry that I did that. I'm sorry that I let my anger get the best of me. Pilar called me from jail, talking about I had her arrested when I would never do such a thing. Listening to her phone call repeatedly, I would have sworn she said in so many words that she was still pregnant. Anyways, I asked Edwina about a statement she made at our wedding, and she told me that she and Bakari were talking, and I lost it. I wanted to hurt him, but after seeing the blood gush from his head, I couldn't stop. What is wrong with me?"

He sighed before replying, "I'm truly disappointed in you, Duke, because you know better. You're the oldest, and you should not have reacted that way."

"I know. I shouldn't have. I'm going to go apologize to him. Grandpa, when you had my dad, how did you feel when you held him? I don't feel connected to this beautiful baby girl. I thought my heart would be pounding out of my chest, but it's not."

"Indescribable indeed."

I nodded my head. I got up, handed him Brielle, and walked out of the room. I was going to Bakari's room. He was only down the hall. Peeking inside his room, I saw that the nurse was pressing a pillow down over Bakari's head. Bursting into the room, I knocked the nurse away.

WHAP!

I backhanded her as hard as I could, and she fell the floor screaming.

"BITCH, IS YOU FUCKING CRAZY? WHAT THE FUCK IS YO' PROBLEM?" I yelled at her.

I was getting ready to kick her when I felt Bakari grab my wrist. His machines were going haywire, and I looked back at him. This was the first time that I had gotten a good look at his face. His shit was fucked up. Very fucked up.

"Duke...I'm sorry," he whispered. "I'm sorry. He's going to kill me!" Bakari's yell was just above a whisper.

"WHO? WHO? WHO'S GOING TO KILL YOU? TELL ME WHO," I yelled at him.

The nurses ran into the room and were trying to move me out the way, but I wasn't budging. I couldn't move until he told me who the fuck was trying to kill him.

"Tell me who the fuck who is trying to kill you," I growled.

"Sir, you have to leave," the nurse kept trying to push me away.

"Duke, tell… tell… Pilar, I'm sorry!" he yelled as loud as he could.

I moved the nurse away again and ran up on him.

"Tell Pilar you're sorry about what? Bakari… who's trying to kill you?"

"Da...Da...."

The machine flat lined, and the security had to drag me out. More nurses ran by with the crash cart as I fell against the wall. My brother was dying right before my eyes because of me. I looked up and saw the nurse that had the pillow over his face walk in the bathroom. I ran into the bathroom after her. She was nursing the bruise that was on her face. She backed against the wall like she could go through it. I grabbed her by her neck and picked her up. I felt my anger rising again.

"What did you do?" I growled. "Why were you trying to kill my brother?"

"Prince… Prince… he… begged me too. I promise," she cried

while raising her hands as if that was going to make me believe her.

"Why would he beg you to kill him?" I squeezed tighter.

"I can't…can't…talk. Let…go," she stuttered.

I let her down, but I kept my hand around her throat.

"He was sleeping. In his sleep, he kept moaning…groaning…I don't know about a girl named Pilar. He kept saying…sorry. He woke up and told me to kill him. He would pay me. I need the money, Prince. I'm sorry. Please believe me," she cried.

"Did he say anything else while he was sleeping?" I asked her.

I let her go, and she slowly slid down to the floor and shook her head. I headed for the door.

"STOP!" she yelled.

"What?" I turned and looked at her.

"Dad, stop. That's… that's…the other thing that he was saying in his dream," she said quietly.

I didn't even know my heart could stop beating and I still be alive.

EDWINA

*H*ave you ever tried to pretend to stay asleep while your husband said he didn't feel a connection with the baby you just had? It was a good thing that the baby had more of my features because I needed him to think that the baby was his for just two more months, but with the way that this shit is unfolding, it seemed like I only had a week or two before everything hit the fan.

See, when I told Duke, I didn't expect that nigga to blow up the way that he did and go bash Bakari's fucking skull in the way that he did. I had slipped inside, away from the drama, and his dad pulled me in his fucking office so fast, asking me what the fuck did I tell Duke for him to react the way that he did. He was screaming at me so loud talking about when I have the baby, he's going to beat my ass because he knows that I been fucking with Bakari. He didn't have any proof because I purposely moved the camera out the view of the guesthouse where I used to meet him. I ain't even know if I should ask about him because I didn't want them to raise their eyebrows at me. Amid the king yelling at me, my water broke, and I ran out just in time to see Duke, Baron, and Bakari behind him. I was so thankful that they didn't hear any of the yelling that was going on in his office.

I wasn't getting out of the hospital for a couple more days because of an infection, so I still had a couple more days to come up with a better plan than the one I had now. It might have to be sooner. Last I checked on their calendars, Duke was going to the States for a few days next week, and on the king's calendar, he had meetings all day on one of those days that Duke was going to be in the States. His brothers, Baron and Bomani, always go with him, and with Bakari fucked up, he wouldn't bother me. I thought it would be easy to sneak away from his annoying ass mothers. *Jesus Christ.*

The lights were low in the room, so I could peek out of one of my eyes. I saw Duke get up and hand the baby to his grandpa. Honestly, his grandpa was the only sane man in this damn family. Well, Duke had a breaking point. He could really be the nicest man in the damn world, but if you said the wrong damn thing or did something stupid, that man will take you out. Once Duke left out of the room, I started breathing a little easier.

While I was laying here in the bed, I concluded that Duke and I were done. I mean, the way that he bashed Bakari's head in was more because his little bitch in the States was in jail and not because he told me. I'm legit glad that I had the baby because I swear, if a nigga will bash his own flesh and blood's head in, he will kill my ass, seriously.

"Edwina… wake up. I know you are not sleeping," his grandpa said.

My heart instantly started beating at a rapid pace. My machine was going off letting me know that my heart had picked up.

"I'm not the one you should be afraid of at this moment," he spoke again.

I could hear him shuffling over to me while I was still pretending to be sleep. He rubbed his hand over my head, and my head instantly yanked back, almost giving me whiplash. My eyes popped open, and Duke's grandpa had the most menacing look on his face.

"Bitch, let me tell you something. Your lil' mothafuckin' ass has come into my family and fucked shit up. I try to let my grandsons think for themselves, and not try to intervene in their lives; but, bitch, you got to mothafuckin' go. You fucking with two of my grandsons, AND their mothafuckin' father. I don't say shit because I mind my damn business and let my sons be grown, but here is it where it ends. You will get your mothafuckin' ass out of this country, and if you breathe a word of this to anybody, I will kill you my mothafuckin' self. I don't care where you go, but you got to get the fuck away from here. Everything that is happening now is your fault," he spoke through gritted teeth.

I swear this is the most that I have ever heard this man talk, and I believed every word that he said. My body was shaking because I was scared out of my mind. I didn't know what I was going to do. The only family that I had was here. I guess he could see the wheels turning in my head.

"Do you understand me?" he growled.

"My parents…they're here," I whispered.

"I don't give a fuck about your parents. You get your ass out of here. The minute they discharge your ass from this hospital, you get the fuck away from here. I don't want you nowhere in the country."

I nodded my head quickly that I understood where he was coming from.

"The baby..."

"The baby stays here," he cut me off.

I instantly started to cry so fucking hard. I needed my baby. He can't just can't take her away from me.

"You take nothing. You leave with the clothes on your back. Again, do I make myself clear?"

I nodded my head because I could not get a word out since I was crying so hard. He walked out the door with my baby. If I could just get to Bakari, he would save me. He loves me. We could leave and start over in another country. The tears slowly stopped and a smile appeared on my face because I knew that Bakari was hooked on this pussy and would do anything to save me.

DUTCH

*F*uck! Fuck! Fuck! This shit was not supposed to happen…
not this way. Duke had been in the room with Edwina around the
clock, and I couldn't get in to see my fucking daughter. Well, I could go
in there, but I wanted to talk to Edwina to make sure that she was okay
since I heard that she had an infection. I was still going to beat the fuck
out of her though. What pissed me off with Edwina was the fact that
her stupid ass was trying to save Bakari from Duke, which let me know
that she probably had been doing more than just talking to his ass.

Duke was smart, but that nigga puts me on a pedestal so he would
never believe any of the shit that I did to Pilar unless Bakari really got
balls enough to tell Duke that he raped his girl. After that beating he
put on Bakari, I'm sure Duke wouldn't believe shit that he had to say
anyway. When I went to visit him in the hospital, he was talking about
how he needed to tell Duke what happened because it's been eating
away at him. He feels sick about what he has done, and all that other
shit. See, I had to let that little sappy ass nigga know that if he even
breathes a word of this shit to Duke, I wouldn't hesitate to kill his ass. I
watched his ass cry like a little ass baby.

Sitting in my office, I was twirling around these stress balls in my
hands. The knock on the door prompted me to put them down.

"Yeah," I called out.

"It's Duke," he spoke on the other side of the door.

I sighed deeply before I pushed the button on my desk to unlock the door. I took my gun out the drawer, took the safety off, and placed it on top of the desk. He walked in slowly with one of his hands behind his back, and he put the other one behind his back. I slowly inched my hand over to my gun. One of his hands fell from behind his back, and I quickly picked my gun up and trained it on him. He didn't say anything but dropped his other hand from behind his back. He wasn't carrying anything, and I instantly felt like shit.

Get it together, Dutch! You acting paranoid. He doesn't know anything, I thought to myself as I felt a little perspiration appear on my forehead.

"Why are you so jumpy, father?" he asked nonchalantly. "It's not like I'm here to kill you or anything like that."

He walked over to my window and looked out over the field. He may not have had a gun in his hand, but he definitely had it in his back.

"What's going on?" I asked.

"Interesting story I got today," he spoke calmly in a monotone voice, like he was a damn professor. "I walked into Bakari's room, and before he went into shock, he told me that someone was trying to kill him. I couldn't really make out who he said was trying to kill him. Do you have an idea of who could want Bakari dead?"

That snitching ass nigga. Damn!

"No…you know he always was in some type of trouble. It ain't no telling who could want him dead."

I wanted to shoot this nigga in the fucking back for looking out the window while talking to me like I was some fucking peasant.

"Interesting," he said while rubbing one of his hands down his wavy ass hair. The was another reason why I knew that nigga belonged to Dame when he was younger.

"Anything else? I'm kind of busy. I'm trying to prepare all of this paperwork and transfer everything over to you. So, you will officially take your rightful place as the king."

"Actually, there is something else," he said, ignoring everything I said about him officially being the king. "A while ago, I got a phone call about Pilar being pregnant. Initially, I was stoked that I was having a baby with the woman that I had planned to spend the rest of my life with, but then, they told me that she was going to have an abortion. I was hurt. Real hurt. So hurt that..."

"Can you kind of speed this along? I really have a lot of work to do," I cut him off.

"No, you don't. Your desk is clear," he replied.

I looked down at my desk, and there was nothing on it. I pulled a file on my desk just to make it seem like I was about to do some work. He didn't do anything but chuckle. This nigga was literally scaring me because of how calm he was being, and he wasn't even looking at me.

"I went and jumped on my jet, hoping that I could catch her before she did. As soon as I pulled up, she was walking out. I snapped. You know I wanted to kill her, but I would miss her too much. As I was getting in my truck, you want to know what she said to me?" he asked and slowly turned to me with his head cocked to the side.

"Whatever she said, I'm sure she's lying. You know I already told you about that broke ass girl and what she will do to get next to your money. She just wants to pull you away from your family, and you know that. Duke, you can't believe her! You're my son, and..."

"What can't I believe her about, father? I never even told you what she said."

"The way you looking at me, I'm sure it was something about me."

"Pilar told me that the reason she got an abortion was because she didn't know who the father was..."

"See. There ya go," I cut him off.

"...because she was raped by you," he finished his statement. "Why would she say that?"

"Duke, that bitch..."

"Careful," he interrupted me and stepped a few steps closer.

"She's lying. She wanted me, and she would do anything to get with me. I told you she just wants the Ramses' money. She'll fuck any Ramses. She said that she will be my mistress. Look," I said.

I pulled out the NDA agreement that I forced her to sign in the hospital and pushed it in front of him. His face didn't change at all.

"I don't have to lie about anything. This what you get for fucking with those city bitches," I said like I proved a point.

"When?" he asked, stroking his beard.

"When what?"

"When did she sign this? She wasn't in Egypt long enough to be alone with you to sign this…unless…"

"Duke, I ain't got to lie to you," I snapped. "You can believe what you want to believe."

"You're right! You're right, Pops. I'm sorry for even questioning you. I know that you would never do anything like that. I just had to ask. All good?"

He held his hand across my desk to shake. I shook it with a good grip. We both stared at each other. While staring in my eyes, he gave me a big smile. He left my office, and I fell back in my chair, letting out a sigh of frustration. He said that everything was all good, but with Duke, you never knew when he was being sarcastic. Only time would tell. If I laid my own son down, you knew I would lay my fucking nephew down.

PILAR

*N*ow that I am about to be a mother, I realized that I had to get some help so I could be a good mom to my twins. I really hadn't been sleeping at night due to stress, so I had an appointment with Dr. Keys to see if I could take anything to get some sleep. I have been stressed because I honestly didn't know how I'm going to take care of these two babies alone. I mean, Duke had given me $40,000, and I only spend some of it to get a car. I roughly have $30,000 left. Babies are expensive. I had to pay for insurance and put back money for their college. There was this Gerber college thing that I read about and they doubled whatever money I put in it, but they would have to go to school in Florida, and I didn't want that. I wanted them to have unlimited options. Basically, I just wanted my kids to have the life that I didn't have.

This pregnancy...I can't explain. When you don't know that you are pregnant, you're fine, but when you find out, you can't keep anything down. Everything that I have tried to eat, comes right back up whether it's morning, noon, or night. I thought that it was only morning sickness. It's probably the damn stress. The most that I have been able to keep down was grilled food. Fried food makes me sick to my stomach. Yeah, these were Duke's kids. That black ass nigga barely ate unhealthily. Getting him to eat something fried was like pulling teeth.

Surprisingly, the doctor's office was not packed. I hated sitting around because these people were staring at me like I was a circus act or something. This was the first time I had been out in public since I had been released from jail. I looked around, and people were starting to whisper. I was about to make a scene, but I was called to the back.

After getting undressed, Dr. Keys walked his fine self into the room.

"Ms. Harrison, how are you doing? How are you adjusting? A few more weeks, and you will be out of your first trimester," he said and smiled at me.

"Well, I can't sleep at all. I couldn't wait to get here so I could ask if there was anything that I could take so I can get some rest. Well, I can get a couple of hours, but after that, I am up again."

"What are some techniques that you have been using to get the little rest that you been getting?" he asked as he rubbed the cold gel on my stomach. I winced at the coolness.

"Well, I eat. Eating normally helps me go to sleep, but I end up watching TV. I have tried looking at the dark ceiling and counting sheep. Nothing is working," I sighed.

"Well, I'm going to give you a list of natural things that you can do to get some sleep. The absolute last thing I want to do is prescribe you any medications. You're not having any headaches or anything?"

Before I could say anything, I heard the babies' heartbeats fill the room.

"There is the first one. Here is the second one. These are some healthy heartbeats, Ms. Harrison."

I was so excited that the heartbeats were healthy that I started crying.

"Pilar, I sense that you have more going on than you want to tell me. So, I'm going to recommend that you go see someone and just talk. These two little ones need a healthy carrier, and if you are not healthy, then these babies won't be healthy. You got that?"

"Yes, I understand."

"Listen, here is the number. She should have some openings for tomorrow. I want to deliver two kids with ten fingers and ten tocs." He laughed.

I took the information, and her name was Savannah Jackson. He cleaned my stomach off, printed out my ultrasound, and left out of the room so I could get dressed. After I was dressed, I went to the front, scheduled another appointment, and left. While I was sitting in the car, I called Savannah's office and scheduled an appointment for tomorrow. I had never seen a therapist before, but just like the doctor said, if she could make my life easier, I would see her.

My phone went off, alerting me that I had a text message. It's funny that every time my phone went off, I thought that it was Duke. I have to get that stupid ass nigga out of my system. When I picked my phone up, the text was from Demarkus.

Demarkus: *Where are you? I need to see you.*

I read over the text message a few times and wondered if I should go see him. I probably shouldn't go see him because I know that he looks at me as more than a friend, and to be honest, our friendship was ruined the day I found him with his wife. Our friendship was even more ruined the night that we had sex. I'm just emotionally unavailable, and I was really not interested in being a side piece to anyone. I deleted the text message altogether.

As I was riding around, I realized that I didn't want to go home, so I ended up at Duke's. I didn't know if I came here to get away or if I wanted to accidently run into him. Who had I become? I never was like this. You know how many niggas I have fucked and ducked, but I just couldn't get this man out of my system? It the babies that got me acting like this. It has to be.

I showed my ID and walked in. It's crazy how live this place is during the day. Duke was an ass. A dummy. A fuck-boy, but he knows how to run a business. I took a seat at the first machine that I saw and started playing.

"Wow! It's nice to see you here. You looking nice!"

I turned around to see Ryder standing there looking just like I saw him when he came into the jail.

"Thank you. You don't look bad yourself. Are you here blowing off some steam? I can only imagine how draining being a lawyer is."

"I'm just here kicking it. I looked up and saw all of that pretty curly hair and immediately knew it was you."

I blushed at his comment. The person next to me had left his seat, and he took a seat next to me. We were facing each other, not even thinking about the machines.

"So, what you do today?" he asked.

"Well, I went to go get these twins checked out, and then I came here. What about yourself?"

"You mind if I touch your little stomach? You can say no if you want to."

I nodded my head, and he started caressing my stomach. It felt so good, especially since the smell of smoke was starting to make me nauseous.

"Well, it's not really anything. It's still soft, and I'll be out of my first trimester in a few weeks. I'm just enjoying this little stomach that I have now. I need to start working out now, so I can snap right back to this size."

"Pilar, you're going to be beautiful anyway. You know that, right? Let your body snap back naturally. Stay off social media, watching those celebrities who have the best doctors and shit."

He had me smiling, and before I could respond, I heard the deep accented voice that I longed to hear.

"If you ain't playing on the machines, then you need to stop taking up my seats…costing this establishment money," Duke spoke through gritted teeth.

We both looked up at him, and I couldn't speak. I hadn't physically seen him since he almost pushed me through the wall of the abortion clinic. The look in his eyes was that of rage, death, and anything synonymous with those words. Ryder stood up and was eye level with Duke. I tried to swallow what felt like a damn lump in my throat.

"Aight, man. There is a better way that you could have said that. I ain't trying to tell you how to run..." Ryder started.

"Then don't. I ain't ask you for yo' mothafuckin' opinion no way," Duke growled.

That left eye was twitching. I wasn't saying Ryder couldn't handle Duke, but I just didn't want to start any shit between my baby daddy and this man.

"You ain't got to be cussin' in front of this young lady. Be respectful."

Ryder...no. Please, no. Duke, keep your mouth closed about us. Please, I thought to myself.

My thoughts were short lived when Duke replied, "Pilar already knows what the fuck this mouth do."

Fuck!

"Pilar, this is your baby..."

"Let's go," I urged Ryder before he completed his question.

I wasn't ready for Duke to know about the babies just yet, and I wanted to tell him myself.

"Yeah, get that nigga out of here. Don't either one of y'all come back," Duke ordered.

Ryder and I started walking toward the door when Duke latched on to the straps of my purse, pulling me back.

"Pilar, don't get that nigga beat the fuck up. You understand me?" Duke whispered in my ear.

"Fuck you, fuck boy!" I snapped.

"Oh, that's where we at now? We back there?"

I can't even believe that he was asking me that stupid ass question. I tried to snatch away from him and ended up breaking the straps on my cheap ass purse. Everything fell out of my purse. I dropped to my knees and quickly tried to shove everything in my purse. Duke put his foot down on a piece of paper and slowly slid it toward him. Duke squatted down and picked up the little black and white picture that held our two little lives on it. It was like time stopped, and everyone around us was frozen but us. Duke stared at the picture, back at me, and back at the picture. He looked back at me, and his eyes had glossed over with a hint of redness.

"Mine?" he asked in a hushed tone.

I gave him a short, quick nod. After that, he got up and walked away from me, leaving me on the ground. He took the ultrasound with him. I scraped everything in my purse and got up. I walked right past Ryder and out the door. I didn't even realize I was crying until Ryder lifted my head up and wiped my tears away.

"Pilar, it'll be alright. No need to cry," Ryder spoke softly.

"I know," I agreed with him.

All I wanted to do was go home, get in the bed, and cry.

∞

"So, that is why my life is one big shit show." I dabbed at the tears that were continuously coming down after telling Dr. Savannah Jackson my whole life story.

She was very attentive and only stopping to ask me to clarify some things. The only thing that I didn't tell her was that I knew who killed Brandon's ass. I just told her that he was killed, and the police think I know who did it.

"Pilar, that is one colorful story, but your life is not a *shit* show. It's just the story of a young girl who had to raise herself and choices that she thought would get her the attention that she deserved from her father. I don't agree with those choices, but you did what you felt was right, and now, we are on the right track to healing. We cannot take the rapes back, but we will help you through this. You won't forget about it, but you are a survivor. I know it doesn't help that your rapist is your children's grandfather..."

"Why do I still love him?" I continued to cry. "I just want to move on from him, but that's not going to be possible. Since he knows about the kids, he is going to want to take care of them. Being around him won't help me get over him. I can't get under one man to get over another one because I'm pregnant, and Duke...is Duke. He would hurt Ryder. Duke is strong; I saw him punch a damn dent in his car."

"You still love him because he was the first guy to have your heart. You still love him because you can't just turn your feelings off for someone no matter what. You have a little while before the babies are born so you won't have to be around him a lot for a while. Even then, Duke can see the kids while you are not around. You don't have to be around him at all while he is seeing the kids unless you think that he is not safe for the children to be around him."

I shook my head slowly because Duke would never hurt our children. He might be an asshole to me, but he would never hurt the kids.

"Pilar, don't hurt Ryder. He seems like a very good guy and has the potential to turn into something more. Pilar, you won't be ready to date for a long time, and you will hurt him."

"What about Demarkus? It's not possible for us to be friends again, is it?"

I already knew the answer to that, but I just wanted to hear it from her for clarification.

"Especially not Demarkus. Let's look at the things that he has done. He lied to you about who he was. Second, he took his job too far, fell for you, and then slept with you. Third, this should have been first, he's married. You can't date a married man nor be friends, especially since there was sex involved."

"You're right," I finally agreed with her after staring at her momentarily.

"Pilar, I never do this, but seeing you once a week won't cut it for me. I'm going to give you my personal number. Guard this number with your LIFE! I want you to text me at any time."

I stored her number in my phone as *SJ*. We scheduled for the same time next week, and I left the office. I felt a little relieved that I could talk to someone that wasn't biased. I guess that was the start of something new.

DUKE

*N*othing prepared me to see Pilar all on the fucking camera letting a nigga rub on her stomach and shit. I was pissed. She better be glad that was the only way that I reacted instead of what I really wanted to do. I couldn't even think the rest of the night. The love of my life was pregnant with my baby…babies. Damn! I was sitting in my home office looking at the ultrasound. I really couldn't believe that Pilar was trying to keep this shit away from me.

Knock! Knock!

"Yeah," I answered.

Mariah pushed the door open with a plate of food. Mariah, my brothers, and I flew over here yesterday, and after Pilar ran out of my place with that nigga on her heels, I been sick. I couldn't eat or sleep.

"Duke, you have to eat something. You haven't eaten anything since last night. Don't worry about Pilar. She is going to come around, you know that. She still loves you," Mariah spoke and sat the plate in front of me. "Can I be honest about something, Duke?"

I nodded my head as I took a piece of food off my plate.

"I really miss her so much. She really had become my best girlfriend, and I've been bored without talking to her. She really loved you. Every time we were together, she talked about you non-stop. She never talked about your money or everything you did for her. She talked about your arrogant ass attitude, and how you fuck her so good. She talked about how you made her feel like she was the most beautiful girl in the world and how she fell so deep in love with you. She is head over heels for you, Duke, and you crushed her. Can you even imagine just a little of how she feels, especially when you didn't believe her? Duke, you didn't even ask one question. You just dismissed her claims."

I looked up at her as I blinked back my tears. I took the time to tell her about the conversation I had with my father. After that nurse told me about Bakari's dream, I knew I had to do something. I had Bakari moved to a hospital over here, and he has had around the clock security that was not to move away from that door no matter who says what. I just had to hear what my dad had to say about those claims that Pilar made. After the first time he got defensive, I knew what Pilar said was true, but I had to play it cool, although I wanted to shoot him between his eyes. After I left his office, I went into my room and cried because I was so pissed that I couldn't off his ass right then and there. How could the nigga that I looked up to for all my life do some fuck shit like that? The nigga that I spent all my life trying to please, raped the woman that I held so fucking dear to my heart, but WHY? He further made himself look guilty the moment he pulled out that NDA agreement, which meant that he had to see Pilar at the hospital. That was the only way.

"I'm so sorry, Duke! Your dad seems like he has a vendetta against you. Every time we go home, and you explain to him what type of new business you opened or plan on opening, he always has to one up you. You remember when he first saw your house, and he said that this house can fit inside of his house five or six times. This house is beautiful, and the average working person cannot afford a place like this," Mariah said.

"You right!"

"Think about it, Duke. Has he ever told you congratulations for anything that you have accomplished or just told you how you could be better? I hope I don't offend you, but your dad is trash. I believe Pilar, and..." she trailed off.

"What, Mariah?"

"Um, I should have told you this a long time ago, but I don't think you would have listened. Your head was so gone over Edwina that... you..."

"Spit it out, Mariah," I growled.

"She fucked your daddy or probably still is fucking him and your brother," she whispered.

"Wait a minute...what?" I looked at her with a confused look on my face.

"Edwina is..."

"Nah, I heard you. I just...just..."

My stomach bubbled, and I threw up what little was in my stomach.

"Duke, I wanted to tell you before you married that bitch, but Baron had come to get you before I could tell you. I hope you forgive me."

"It's all good. I probably would have told you to mind your business anyway. I mean, I knew you didn't like her, but I just thought it was because she didn't like you."

"I guess you right," she said, turning to leave out of the room.

I grabbed my keys and left my house. I had to go talk to Pilar. I knew I was going to have to do a lot of begging to get back in her good graces. I just wanted to apologize. Moments later, when I pulled into the parking lot, I noticed that she had bought a little raggedy car that would be upgraded when my fucking kids got here. Ain't no way the mother of my kids was going to be riding in some shit like that. I saw Baron's car parked there as well. As soon as I knocked on the door, Swan opened it with an attitude.

"What the hell you want?" Swan asked with her hands on her hips.

"Aye, girl, if you don't let my bro in this fucking house, I know something," Baron said from the couch.

"Yeah, watch out," I said, moving her out the way.

I dapped my brother up and went to knock on Pilar's door. She opened the door slightly and then slammed it, and I heard the locks on the door.

BOOM! BOOM!

I bammed on the door as hard as I could.

"Pilar Renee, if you don't open this fucking door, I swear to God, I'll knock it off the hinges," I said.

BOOM! BOOM!

"PILAR, YOU ARE NOT GOING TO..."

She opened the door in the middle of my sentence. She turned and walked away from the door. She sat on the bed and focused on the TV. I was totally surprised that she was not naked since she rarely had on clothes. She had on a Calvin Klein sports bra with matching briefs. Her stomach wasn't big, but I could tell that something was there. God, this woman was fucking gorgeous. If I didn't get her out of this house, I would be begging her to fuck, and I was not trying to be on that.

"Do you want to..." I started.

She got up, ran to the bathroom, and I heard her puking up the contents of her stomach. I walked in and held her hair back for her.

"How are you feeling? I thought pregnant people only get morning sickness."

"Well, that's a damn lie. I have been having morning, afternoon, and night sickness. I'll be out of my first trimester soon, so hopefully, this throwing up shit will be history."

"Well, I guess me taking you out for a cup of juice is non-existent, huh?"

"I don't feel well, so maybe another day."

"I really want to talk to you. Can we just walk along the beach, so if you need to throw up, you can throw up in the sand or something?" I laughed.

She raised her eyebrow at me and then rolled her eyes at me. She got up and went in her closet. She came out with a pair of leggings, and a long-sleeved shirt. I watched her get dressed, and slide in her shoes.

She put on one of my hoodies and walked by me out her bedroom door. I followed behind her, and we both could hear Baron and Swan fucking. That nigga was moaning like a bitch, and I couldn't wait to get on his ass about it. I made sure Pilar locked the front door, and we walked across the street to the beach.

The waves crashing against the shore sounded nice. We were both quiet while walking. I guess since I asked to talk to her, I could start the conversation, but I just wanted to be in her presence. Naturally, my hand gravitated to hers, and she didn't resist.

"Are you gon' talk?" she asked.

"Yeah... yeah, I am. Um, Pilar, I really wish I knew how to say this, but I don't. Can you tell me what happened? The night that...you know."

"Which night?"

"Don't play with me. The night my father...you know."

"WHICH...NIGHT?"

I yanked her around to face me. I lifted her face up toward me. The moon was bright enough to where we could see each other.

"Pilar, don't fucking play with me. Why the fuck is you saying which night?"

"Well, your nasty ass father raped me twice. The second time was with his son, Bakari. I know you look up to that guy, but he's really not a nice man." She snatched away from me and continued to walk.

"I woke up after our fight, handcuffed to the bed, with your dad's hands between my legs. He raped me, pissed on me... on my face, and tried to piss in my mouth but only a little got in. He kicked me in my ribs after I wouldn't open my mouth. He asked me to be his mistress and said that you didn't give a shit about me because you knew that he said he would kill me if you brought me to Egypt," she cried. "Is that true, Duke?" she whispered. "Did your dad tell you that he would kill me if I came to Egypt?"

I couldn't even talk after the vile things that Pilar said my dad did to her. The lump was so big, that I really had to take a break. I sat down in the sand while Pilar stood next to me.

"Yes...yes, that is true. I never thought...thought you would leave the hotel. This is all my fault. Everything. I should have just told you the truth from the beginning. I'm sorry," I cried into my hands.

"The second time, I had just come from a date, and..."

"A date?"

"I was grabbed and woke up in a room handcuffed to a bed again. I woke up to Bakari and your father talking. I can't remember what they were saying. I told your father that he was obsessed with me. He asked me to be his mistress again, and that's when the rape started. Bakari was resistant, and your dad basically called him a pussy. While he was...was inside of me... he whispered in my ear, and he told me that he didn't want to do it. I told him that he wasn't a man, and that's when the assault started, and that is the last thing that I remembered before I woke up with you and that man arguing over me."

Getting on my knees and grabbing her around her waist, I cried into her stomach. I felt so fucking bad for it. I guess that's why Bakari kept telling me to tell Pilar that he was sorry. I looked up at her and met her gaze.

"Pilar, I'm so sorry! Please forgive me…please forgive me."

"I don't know! Not yet, Duke. The love I had for you was left back in that auditorium when you made me look like a fool. The only man I ever fell in love with is married to another woman," she spoke. "I honestly don't think we can come back from that. I'm sorry," she cried and pulled away from my embrace.

Leaving me on my knees, she ran back down the beach, and I'm sure she went back home. I couldn't even ask the Lord what I did to deserve this because I knew exactly what I did. I played with two hearts. That would have to be put on the back burner because my first order of business was killing my dad and beating Bakari's ass again to the point where he would wish he was dead.

EDWINA

*W*hen I was discharged from the hospital, they offered me a wheelchair, but I didn't take it. I went to the front and asked for Bakari's room, but they said that there wasn't a Bakari occupying a room at the hospital. I had her check again, and she told me the same thing she told me the first time. She said that he was moved, but that was all that they could tell me. I tried to use my phone, but my phone was turned off.

"Fuck," I mumbled under my breath.

I was getting more and more frustrated as the time went on. I didn't have a phone to call me a cab. I looked in my purse and saw a couple hundred dollars.

"Hi, sorry to bother you again, is there an ATM machine nearby?" I asked the receptionist.

"Two blocks down," she replied like she was annoyed.

I walked outside with this big ass bag. I tried to blend in like a normal person. I wrapped my face up a little more because I didn't want people to notice me and start asking questions or get in my face with those damn annoying ass cameras. I haven't had to walk this far in so long that I was literally drained by the time I made it to the ATM

Machine. Not to mention, I just gave birth to a seven-pound baby.

In my wallet, I had about ten of Duke's cards. I stuck the first one in and tried to withdraw some money, but there was nothing. I couldn't get shit out. I tried each of the cards and nothing. I was on the last card, and I silently prayed to God that I would be able to get some money but nothing. They had cut my damn cards off.

"AHHHHHH!" I screamed out and banged on the machine. I leaned my head against the machine and blew a sign of frustration.

I thought about all the money that I had put in the different safe deposit boxes and the account that I had in my grandmother's name. I walked all the way to the bank, and by the time I made it inside, I was a sweaty mess, and I knew I smelled horrid because I could smell myself. I signed in under a different name.

"Meagan Elizabeth," the lady called out from the back.

I got up and walked into her office. She turned her nose up as soon as I walked in her office. I had to ignore it because I ain't want to cause a scene and get put out the bank. I showed her my ID, and bank account information.

"I want to withdraw from the account in my grandmother's name. It was…you know…mad money," I whispered.

She typed on the computer and shook her head at the same time. She typed for like five minutes straight without saying a word.

"I'm sorry, Mrs. Ramses, but that account was closed a few days ago by your grandfather-in-law," she said while shaking her head.

"No, that can't be right. He didn't have access to that account.

How did he know about that account?" I demanded.

I was pissed because it was well over a million dollars in that account. I opened that account for this sole purpose, and now all of it is gone. I rubbed my temples to combat the headache that I was getting.

"Ma'am, I didn't close this account. So, I really can't help you. Is there anything else that I can help you with?"

"Yes, I have safe deposit keys, and I would like to go into them."

"What are the numbers?"

I wrote down the numbers for her, and she told me to follow her. I wrote my name down on a clipboard and followed her to the door. I had to stay outside while she got all the boxes out. After she got out the boxes out, she invited me in, left, and locked me inside. I opened the first box, and it was nothing but a piece of paper. I picked it up and read the words on it.

"You got to be quicker than that," I read aloud.

It wasn't signed, and I didn't know who it was from. It had to be from Duke, Bakari, or Dane.

All the boxes had the same note in it except for the last one. The last one had several stacks of money, a passport, and a note.

This is only because Duke wouldn't have wanted you to be assed out. Take this money, leave, and never come back. If I even think you are back in this country, I will kill you my mothafuckin' self. GDR.

GDR had to mean Grandpa Dane Ramses. I stuffed the contents of the box in my bag except for the passport. I knocked on the door to let the woman know that I was done. I gave her the keys since I would no longer be using them. I walked out the bank. I stared at the passport for a while and wondered where the hell I would go, and then I got a bright idea. Every other plan that I had failed, but this wouldn't. See, Duke may not have given a damn about me, but I knew for a fact who he gave a damn about. If I couldn't live a happy life, then neither could Duke, and I knew exactly what to do.

"I always wanted to go to the United States," I said to myself.

BAKARI

*S*tupid. *Selfish. Ungrateful. Unappreciative. Foolish. Jealous.*

Those are all the words that I could use to describe myself at this moment. Here I was, laid in a hospital bed, saved by the one person that I had hated on the most…Duke. When my dad made us come over here with Duke, I was excited. I loved all my brothers, but when you go through your whole life hearing *'You should be more like Duke. Duke was so smart. Duke was one of the best students I ever had'* it takes a toll on you. That's all I heard all throughout my high school and college career. Hell, Duke never played a sport in school, but the coaches would be like *'I bet Duke can play ball better than that.'* It got to the point where I started to hate my brother. It was really nothing he did to me, but it was how hard he made it for me. Everybody always wanted me to live up to Duke's potential, and it made me sick to my stomach. The people that I tried to talk to always said that it sounded like I was hating, but I wasn't.

My brother couldn't dumb himself down. I even transferred colleges after a year or so, but I still heard the shit. Baron and Bomani sucked all that fame up. They said that's how they got the majority of their hoes. I ain't want to get no hoes off Duke's name, but that's what it always seemed like. This nigga was low key but was still loved by many. Duke was one of the nicest people in the world, but if you got on that nigga bad side, you would much rather be dead. Case and point, that nigga banged my damn head against that plate, damn near killing me, and I was his damn brother.

The thing with Edwina… it just happened and kept happening. I was addicted to her. Her pussy was intoxicating. I take it as that I was younger than her, and that was my first time dealing with an older woman. The more we fucked, the more I resented Duke. He didn't have one clue. Honestly, I didn't mean to get her pregnant. The rubber broke, and her ass got pregnant. I never hit her raw until she was already pregnant. When he met Pilar… her beautiful ass…he forgot all about Edwina. I would be laying in the bed with her when he would call, and they would only talk for like five minutes before he would rush her off the phone. I felt bad for her. At first, she would cry, but she thought that Pilar was just Duke's US fling but figured out they were much more, and that's when she started changing up.

I knew that she had the baby, and I wondered if Duke knew that her baby was mine. He couldn't have known that the baby belonged to me since he had moved me over to the States. I was ready to be discharged since I'd been in hospital beds for the last two weeks. They have been running test after test on me. A part of me wanted to know what Duke was going to do when he put two and two together regarding the baby and regarding me raping Pilar. I shuddered at the thought of that. I hadn't really talked to my dad since then. He was foul as fuck for that shit. I ain't never had to rape no bitch, and I never wanted to start. That was my sole purpose of asking Edwina if my dad had ever raped her. I hated rapist, and I had become one.

I was looking at the TV when the door came open.

"Clear the room," Duke ordered.

My security cleared the room quick as hell. My heart instantly started beating fast. I hated that these damn machines picked up everything because I was sure that the machines alerted him that I was scared. Duke pulled a seat up next to my bed, turned the chair around, and sat in it. He rested his arms across the back of the chair and glared at me.

"You know, Bakari," he said and pulled a gun from under his hoodie and held it in his hands. "The only reason that you are not dead is because our grandfather needs us back home in a couple of days," he said and pulled the silencer out.

"I talked to Pilar." He screwed the silencer on the gun. "She told me some things that really pissed me off, and I really mean pissed me off."

His tone was so menacing that it would scare anyone who was listening.

"So, I'm going to ask you one time and one time only…why? My advice to you is that you better just answer the question."

I was so scared because, in the back of my mind, I really did want to say why what? I didn't know what he knew, but since he said that he talked to Pilar, I was going to assume that he is talking about that shit that our dad made me do. He stood up and placed the cold steel against my head, and I damn near pissed myself.

"Um, our dad…Dad…he made me," I stuttered. "I never wanted to hurt Pilar…"

"Bullshit, you didn't like Pilar since the first day you laid eyes on her. Why am I supposed to believe that you didn't do that shit because you wanted to?" he cut me off.

"Duke, I swear to God! I was pissed that Dad made me do that shit. I even told her that I was sorry for doing that shit. He was calling me a pussy."

"So, who gives a damn about being called a damn pussy, Bakari? Who?"

"He would have killed me."

"So, you raped a girl because you were afraid that you were going to be killed. Bakari, you would have died a man. Now, you're going to die a pussy ass rapist."

Click!

He pulled the trigger on the gun, the gun clicked, and I screamed like a bitch. I felt the warm liquid running down my leg and shit come out of my ass. I pissed and shitted on myself like a bitch. Duke fanned his nose while laughing. See, this was the crazy shit that I was talking about. He laughed at the craziest shit, and I was convinced that my brother was a psychopath.

"When I kill you, it's going to be slow and painful, or…"

Click!

He pulled the trigger on the gun again, and I screamed again. He laughed again. He twisted the silencer off the gun, put it back in his pocket, and slipped the gun back on his side.

"Now, clean yourself up. We have a flight to catch," he commanded.

I nodded my head, but my mind was on the thing that he said before telling me to get cleaned up. He said...*when* he killed me.

GRANDPA DANE

My family was destroyed beyond repair because of women, Edwina and Pilar. Edwina fucking two of my grandsons and my son. Pilar got my future king's head gone. The way that he threw that crown at Bakari the day of his wedding, I knew then, that it would come down to him choosing between his crown or that girl, and the bad part of that is that I don't know which one he's going to choose. I try to stay out of all my kid's business, but after Duke made a spectacle of himself on live TV, I figured I had to step in, so these men can get this shit off their chest like grown men.

Dutch was always different than his twin Dame. I missed my son every day, and I couldn't help but to think what life would be like if he was king instead of his brother. I never thought that my son would be the one to rape girls. Now, when Bakari broke down and told me that shit, I wanted to kill him on sight because that was not what we were about. He let the power go to his head, and I couldn't help but think that I gave him his crown to early, and I was strongly regretting it.

I found out about Bakari and Edwina because I was going to the guest house to get something out the bathroom, and I heard them moaning and groaning like they weren't expecting anybody to bring their asses over there. I found out about Edwina and my son when they

79

thought they were slick, sneaking off the day that Duke damn near sent Bakari to meet his maker.

"You think this sit down is going to help?" Constantine asked as I got dressed for this meeting with my son, and grandsons. She was rubbing little Brielle's hair. She had a head full of hair and was as cute as a button. It was a shame that her mom was a slut. I kissed her on her nose, and she stirred.

Constantine was the absolute love of my life. When I first laid eyes on her, I knew that she was going to be my wife. My dad and grandad had multiple wives, but that was never my thing. We only had two kids, and that was more than enough for me. We were going to take care of Brielle until we got our son and grandsons straightened out.

"Baby, I honestly don't know. I sent that gal away, though. She is to never be seen again unless she wants her head on a chopping block," I said as I slipped on my shoes.

She gave me a kiss, and I kissed Brielle again and headed downstairs to the basement. When I made it down to the basement, they were all sitting in their respective chairs. It was quiet as a mouse, but the tension was so thick that you couldn't cut it with a butcher knife. It was at this very moment that I knew that having a regular conversation was out of the picture.

"Bomani, do you have those things that I told you to get?" I asked him.

"Yes, sir. I do! Do you need them right now, or you want me to take them to the groundskeeper?"

"No, I need them now. Can you get them for me, please?"

Bomani put the collars on the table along with the machines that go with them.

"What the heck are those? Dog collars?" Duke laughed.

"Yes. You guys have been acting like animals lately, so I thought that it would be fitting for this conversation that we are about to have," I replied.

I grabbed one of the collars and placed one on Duke's neck. I placed the other ones on Bakari and Dutch's neck.

"Wait, why Baron and Bomani get to sit this one out? This ain't fair," Duke huffed.

"Baron and Bomani seem to act like they are the only ones that got some damn sense in this family. So, no, they are not going to wear one," I replied to him. "Bomani, test them out for me. Level one, please."

He pressed the button on each machine, and they all groaned at the shocks that were going through their body. I hated to have to do this to my son, and grandsons, but I felt like this was the only thing that was going to keep them in their seats while the other one was talking. I started walking around the table while they were all looking at me.

"So, do anybody want to go first? I know we all would like to be somewhere other than here," I asked while walking continuously making circles around the table.

"What is it that you think we got to talk about, Grandpa?" Duke asked.

"Get whatever off your chest, and whatever is said is going to be left down here in the basement. When we emerge from this basement, we are going to go back to being the nice and lovely family that we were before all this drama took place," I replied.

At least that is what I hoped that would happen, but some of these crimes are unforgivable, even for the nicest man.

"Well, I guess I'll go first. I don't really have much to say, but what I will say is that what Dutch and his son, Bakari, did is punishable by death, and that is the end of it," Duke shrugged.

"Duke..." Bakari started.

"Nah, I ain't trying to hear shit, Bakari. If that man had of threatened to kill you because you didn't want to rape a girl, you should have died, and that's the end of it," Duke addressed Bakari. "I'll never be able to look at you as a father again, Dutch," Duke addressed him.

"Duke, I'm sorry! I'm so sorry! Please...forgive me. I don't want to die."

"Nigga, you think I give a fuck about you addressing me as your father. I don't, because guess what, I ain't your fucking pappy anyway. Your pappy is..."

Shit!

"Dutch," I interrupted him.

"Nah, Pops, we putting it all out there, then let's fucking do it. Your pappy is dead. He died before you were born. That fuck nigga fucked my girl...your mom and got her pregnant. See, Duke, I ain't never liked you for that sole purpose alone," he growled.

Duke rose out of his seat, and I cued Bomani to shock the shit out of Duke, and he sat back down. This conversation had turned ugly, and I knew when Duke got to the point of no return, that shock collar wasn't going to help.

"You are the spitting image of him, down to that stupid ass birthmark on your back. He always got everything he wanted with that *fucking charming personality.* He got all the girls and even had women on his fucking jock. You're just like him. For that, I hate you. Everything you touched, I touched. Your precious, Edwina...I was her first, and she had MY baby," he snapped.

Everybody looked at Duke for a reply, but he just sat there not saying a word, which was not good. Everybody focused their attention on Bakari when he spoke.

"On the contrary, Dutch, Edwina had MY baby," he addressed his father and looked at Duke. "I never meant for this to happen. I swear I didn't. We just happened. I swear, and then it kept happening. I never meant to hurt you."

Duke still didn't say anything. Nothing. It's like everybody in the room was waiting for a reply from him, but nothing.

"Duke...bro, say something," Baron coached, but he still ain't say shit.

He wasn't even bothered by Bakari, he just kept staring at Dutch, who was now staring at Bakari like he had three heads on his shoulders.

"As far as that bitch, Pilar...yeah, I raped her...twice. I loved it, and I would do it again if I could," Dutch admitted.

Duke was squeezing on the arms of the chair hard as hell, and I gave Bomani the signal to get ready to turn that shit up as far as it could go.

"The way she struggled under me made my dick get harder and harder. Calling out for you pissed me off further and further. Her pussy was so fucking tight, even after fucking all those niggas. You're in love with a hoe, Duke. I don't even know why you mad. I took so much pleasure in releasing my piss all over..."

Duke leaped out of that chair and dove right on to Dutch. He was no match for Duke, especially when he got angry. Duke was raining down blows on his face so fast, and hard.

"BOMANI, TURN IT UP! TURN IT UP!" I yelled at him, while Baron was trying to pull him off Dutch.

"GRANDPA, I AM! I AM! I AM!" he shrieked back at me.

Duke reared back and snatched that collar off with one good yank and continued to rain his blows down on him. Baron was finally able to pull him off Dutch while it took Bomani and Baron to hold him back. Dutch got up with hardly any teeth in his mouth and blood pouring from every part of his face. We all stood and stared at him.

"So what? It's all y'all against me? The one that took care of each and every one of y'all," Dutch said while pointing at each of the boys.

The room fell silent as everybody stared at him until Bomani started speaking.

"Honestly, Dad, Duke raised us. Well me. I was ten when you made me go with Duke to the States. It was him who made sure I was fed and even tucked me in at night. It was him who stayed up with me, teaching me how to speak English and making sure I got my homework done. Bakari, you too. Your betrayal hurts the worst. What your scholarships didn't cover, Duke paid out of his own pocket. His business wasn't pulling in the money it was when he paid for that shit, but you didn't know that, did you? He damn near went bankrupt trying to drop that $50,000 for you to go to school that year you lost your scholarship. See, now you looking stupid. The amount of shit this nigga has done for us that WE don't even know, and the way you repay him is by sleeping with his girl, AND getting her pregnant," Bomani said, and his voice started trembling. "Bakari, what the fuck is your problem? The only vendetta you should have is the one against your father. The one who made you rape a girl."

"Shut the fuck up, Mani. You don't know how it feels to be compared to that nigga all the time. *Duke this...Duke that*," Bakari snapped.

"Who gives a damn? You just trying to make excuses for being a wack ass nigga. That should have motivated your ass to do better. I ain't give two fucks about a nigga or bitch talking to me about my brother. Hell, I'm proud that this nigga is my brother. When folks used to talk shit to me about my brother. Guess what? I said, 'Where your rich brother at?' You foul, Bakari, and that's all there is to it," Baron said.

Dutch started laughing, and we all focused back on him. Baron and Bomani had to start holding Duke back again because there was absolutely nothing funny about this moment.

"That was the same way I felt about Dame. Everybody always compared me to Dame. We had damn near the same face, and I was still getting called the weird one, but I fixed that though!"

I walked closer to him and asked him to clarify what that meant. Bakari kind of got in front of me.

"You smart. You already know what that mean." Dutch grinned a toothless smile.

"You telling me…that you killed my son. Your brother?"

He didn't say anything. I became weak and had to sit down. It's been decades since my son drowned, and the pain never gets easier. I pulled my phone out and called my security down to the basement. Moments later, my whole security team was in the basement with their weapons drawn.

"Look at you! You never cared about me. Everything was always about your precious little Dame. You never paid any attention to me. Dame was your fucking golden child. That's why I took pleasure in watching him drown. While you had me in swimming lessons, you should have had Dame in there instead of parading him around town," he blurted out as he was being led out. "Duke, you next," he claimed. Duke didn't even bother to address him.

"Please, take Dutch into the dungeon and don't give him anything until I figure out what to do with him," I told my head security guy. "Also, strip him."

They led him out the basement, and I told all my grandsons to have a seat. They all were staring at me to continue. I'm sure they had so many questions. I got up and went over to one of the shelves, and pulled out a box of pictures. I retrieved pictures of both Dame and Dutch and walked back over to the table. I put the pictures in the middle of the table as they slid them around and looked at them.

"Dang, Duke…You look just like…Dame!" Bomani said, and Duke didn't even budge.

"Duke, I can assure you that I never even knew about Dame being your father. When you were born, you looked exactly like him, and I never questioned it. I thought that God was maybe just giving me a piece of Dame back. Your demeanor is just like him. Your wit. Your everything is a mirror of Dame, and I never even put two and two together. We never told you about Dame because it hurt your grandmother to talk about him. She still hasn't moved on and probably never will. Losing a child never gets easier."

"Where is Edwina?" Duke asked.

"I don't know. I sent her away. I didn't want to kill her because I ain't know how you would feel about me killing your wife. Briclle is with your grandmother. She has money, and she will be fine. Obviously, she is smart since she played three niggas under the same roof."

There was an awkward silence in the room.

"Look, guys. It's apparent that you guys' relationship will never be the same, but is there any way that we can restore some type of normalcy back into the family? Duke, I'm not asking you to forgive Bakari today or tomorrow, but is there something that he can do for you to spare his life for now?"

Duke didn't say anything but continued to bite his bottom lip. The same thing that Dame used to do when he was thinking about something.

"I'll ask Pilar what she thinks I should do regarding Bakari. It's really no question on what's going to happen to Dutch. It's over with for him, Grandpa, and that's it. Dad, uncle, whoever…he will die by my hands."

"Well, there is nothing else that I can say to that," I replied. "Gentlemen, let me have the room, please. Duke, you stay."

I watched my grandsons leave the room, and I focused on Duke.

"So, how is Pilar doing?"

"Well, she's pregnant…with twins, and I wondered where the twins came from because she doesn't have twins in her family. She's okay, but she doesn't want to be with my anymore. She told me she doesn't know when she's going to forgive me, and I'm hurt. I truly never thought that my dad would do something like that, and now I really feel like an ass for not believing her."

"She's going to come around, but there is something else that I want to discuss with you. Are you still going to take on the task of being the king? After learning that he raped Pilar, I considered that a flagrant, and I have revoked his crown, effective immediately."

"I'm really honored, Grandpa, but right now, being king is the furthest thing from my mind. Maybe I'll be able to answer you soon, but not right now. I just want to focus on getting my family back," he said before he got up and left me alone with my thoughts.

The thing that I battled with now, was how was I going to tell Constantine that her son was murdered by her other son, and most importantly, that Duke was going to kill him. I wanted to kill him because of that revelation he made about killing Dame, but I knew that Duke was going to make his death much worse than what I could ever do.

PILAR

I hadn't seen or talked to Duke since that day on the beach, and that's been almost two weeks ago. After my session with Savannah last week, she told me that I should try and have a dinner with my grandfather. I was kind of pissed with her when she said that shit, because if I'm not going to give my sperm donor a chance, then why should I give that nigga a chance. They both been knowing at me, and never made an effort until now to try and get to know me. I took the liberty of calling and telling him that I would meet him for lunch so we could talk. I didn't know what we were going to talk about though. I'd just let him ask me questions.

I pulled into the crowded restaurant and walked inside. He stood up and waved me over. I smiled a little at him wearing his uniform. He looked nice. He stood up to hug me, but I sat down, rejecting his hug. We stared at each other momentarily.

"So, thank you for meeting me today," he finally said. "I don't know what changed your mind, but thank you!"

"It's all good! So, why you looking all nice and shit?" I asked.

"Well, I had to do a press conference today regarding the shooting of that young man, Brandon. His girlfriend won't leave us alone about it. She comes to the office every day asking if we had a lead."

"Well, I hope you don't use this lunch to try and get answers out of me because that ain't what this lunch is for. I actually only scheduled this lunch because my therapist advised me to."

"Pilar, if you know who did this, why won't you say anything? If someone killed someone you love, wouldn't you want someone to come forward with some information?"

"Please refer to what I just said before you said what you said, sir. I'm really not going to say it again."

"Alright! So, tell me something about yourself," he said, changing subjects.

"Well, what don't you know already? If you knew I lived here, I'm sure you know..." I trailed off as I thought about what Savannah said.

Be open minded, Pilar. Don't be defensive. Listen to everything that he has to say.

I took a deep breath before starting again, "Well, I graduated high school and went to Jackson State University and got a degree in Health Sciences. Moved here, and thought everything was going to be good, and I ended up working at a gas station. I got fired from there, and thankfully, my baby daddy is rich or I would have had to start back having sex for money," I said as I took a sip of my water.

He sat there looking at me crazily while I told the waitress my order. I made sure to order a small salad because you never knew when these damn twins would start acting up and make me run to the bathroom and throw up. He ordered his food, and after the waitress left, he stared at me. His face softened up, and I could tell that he had so many questions.

"Please, don't feel sorry for me. I'm good. I'm over it. Well, at least I thought I was over it until I got in therapy and had to relive all that shit over again."

"I mean, but..." he started, and I raised my hand to stop him.

"There really are no buts. Had *you* done what *you* were *supposed* to do as a man, my mother would have still been a drug addict, my piece of shit sperm donor, would have still been a piece of shit. This is just how life works. That is how I fed myself, and I don't regret any of it. So, let's move on," I spoke.

"Well, I really don't know what else to say. You literally left me speechless after that. So, maybe you can guide the conversation."

"I'm really not sure what I want to know about you, to be honest."

Before he could reply, I heard someone say his name.

"Robert, you got me traveling all over the city during lunch time, and...oh, who is this?" She stood at the end of the table.

I looked up and stared directly into my grandma's face. Not my grandma but her sister. My stomach started to turn, and I rubbed my stomach to try and get the twins to settle down. If my grandma didn't drink and smoke herself to death, her face wouldn't have had has many wrinkles as it did before she died. Her teeth wouldn't have been stained, and she wouldn't have had a beer belly. Her face would have aged gracefully just like Lenita's.

"You're not calling me here to tell me that you got a little hussy pregnant, are you?" his wife said while looking at me pat my stomach.

Strike one.

"No, worse," I replied.

"Pilar, I hope you don't mind that I invited my wife to lunch. I wanted her to meet you."

"Meet me for what? This is one of your little charity cases that you work with during this time of year?"

Strike...two.

I pressed my lips together and smiled at her because this old bitch didn't know how close she is to getting cursed the fuck out. Just one more remark...one more, and it's going to be on in this restaurant.

"Lenita, please just sit down so I can talk to you damn!" Robert snapped.

"I don't want to sit down until you..." she started.

"Look, bitch! Just sit the fuck down, damn! You are irritating the fuck out of me, and when I become irritated, my twins become irritated, which makes it worse for you. I'm not pregnant by him nor am I some *charity* case. Sit down or leave. At this point, I would prefer the latter."

She slowly slid her ass into the seat and started sipping on his water. She had an attitude, but I didn't give a damn because I didn't tear into her as much as I wanted to or should have. She probably needed a humbling experience anyway.

Robert turned to her with a solemn look on his face. I rolled my eyes to the ceiling. This nigga was scared to tell his wife about something that happened decades ago. Her ass was probably lacking in bed, and that's why he cheated on her. Robert claimed he was drunk, but please, any fool with some common sense knew that you don't put yourself in situations knowing that you will fuck up if you get drunk. He wanted to fuck my grandma. End of story. He just used being drunk as an excuse. I wasn't new to the game.

"Robert, what are you about to tell me? You need to spit it out because I am getting nervous. You acting like you are cheating on me or something?"

I started rubbing my temples out of frustration. See, I ain't never been the one to beat around the bush. If I got something I need to tell you, then that's what the fuck I'm going to do. You either going to be mad or let it ride. Either way, it ain't no beating around the bush.

"Years ago..."

"Forty-two years to be exact," I said, hoping that I could speed this along.

She cut her eyes at me and then focused back on Robert. Damn, my mom would have been forty-two had she not stuck that last needle in her arm.

"Robert, spit it out."

"I…I slept with Lenora, and Cisco was my daughter. This is my… our granddaughter, Pilar Harrison."

I waved and gave her a little smile. Her eyes were welling up with tears, and I prayed that she didn't get dramatic.

"Why? Why did you sleep with her? I always knew you were attracted to her. How many times?"

"I was drunk, and it just happened."

She dabbed at the few tears that had slid down her face.

"So, what does she want from us. Money? Take care of those children? What? She's not getting anything from us," she spoke.

Strike three.

"First of all, I don't want jack shit from you nor him, lady. It was him who had people pretending to be my friend for whatever reason. It was him who sent lawyers to help me out when I didn't need it. I ain't ask him for shit, nor will I ever. Second, the real reason he cheated was because you are a self-centered bitch, and he didn't want you. He wanted my grandma, but she wouldn't have fit into his life the way it is now. You probably found some way to trap him, and that's why he stayed. Third, I let you get away with calling me a hussy and a charity case, so you better be glad I ain't smacking the shit out of you right now. So, with that being said…" I scooted my chair back from the table and stood up. "Robert, it was really nice to see you, but I don't need this extra stress in my life right now. Don't contact me, and I won't contact you," I said and walked away.

I didn't even give Lenita the satisfaction of acknowledging her again after that. I went out to my car and dug my phone out of my purse to text Savannah.

Me: Lunch went bad. Need to smoke.

SJ: No. We will talk about the lunch at the next session.

Me: Need to have sex. I'm frustrated.

SJ: No.

Me: Why you keep saying no to everything? Those are the only two things that help me cope. Sex and smoke. One of them is happening today.

SJ: No. Go write.

Me: Settle for oral, okay?

SJ: NO!

I threw my phone down in the cup holder and drove home. Between my frustration and the traffic, I was pissed the fuck off to the point where I just started crying. Amid me crying, my phone rang. I picked it up without even looking at the caller ID.

"WHAT?" I screamed into the phone.

"Pilar, are you okay? Why are you screaming and crying?" the voice asked on the phone.

Pulling the phone back, I looked at the name across the screen, and it was Ryder. I tried to straighten myself up and respond to this question. I couldn't believe that he was calling me since that fiasco with Duke at his damn place of business.

"Um, I'm just a little frustrated that's all."

"You want to talk about it? You can come to my office. I'm finishing up some paperwork. I would love to listen," he said.

"Okay. Send me the address, so I can put it in my GPS system," I said and hung up the phone.

Moments later, my phone dinged, and it was the address. His office was twenty minutes away. Speeding like a mad woman through traffic, I cut the drive in half. His office was in a fancy building. I cleaned my face up and walked inside the building. There was a girl sitting at the front desk, and I could already tell that she was about to give me attitude.

"We don't do donations, ma'am," the woman said as soon as I stepped to the front desk.

I looked down at myself to make sure I ain't look homeless or something, since Lenita's ass assumed I was a charity case too. I had on a simple pair of blue jeans, a plain t-shirt, and a pair of Jordan slides. I didn't look homeless; I looked fucking comfortable.

"Do I look I need a donation? I'm looking for Ryder's office," I said, cocking my head to the side.

Her focus changed when I asked about Ryder, which was an automatic sign of her wanting him and couldn't have him or already fucked him, and he didn't want to fuck her anymore.

"Um, he doesn't have any appointments. He's at lunch," she replied with an attitude.

"I know. I'm here for his *lunch*. Can you direct me to his office, or do I have to call him?"

She squinted her eyes at me.

"Pilar, there you are. I was getting ready to call you to make sure you found us okay," Ryder said, approaching me. "My office is right here."

I followed him to his office, which was to the left of her desk. As soon as we walked in his office, I walked to his opened blinds. I licked my tongue out at her before I snapped the blinds closed.

"Aha, I see you have met Jennifer. Don't worry, she's mean to everyone," he said after I turned around.

"Nah, she wants to fuck you or something," I said as I took a seat in front his big desk, much like the one in Duke's office.

Duke...don't think about Duke.

"So, tell me what has the little baby so mad that she picked up the phone screaming."

"Well, I had lunch with Robert, and it didn't go so well when I met his wife. She treated me like I wanted money from them or something, when that was not the case. I had to curse her out when she kept talking shit. Then I got frustrated and left the lunch. When I get frustrated, I smoke, or I have sex or both. That is how I cope. I texted my therapist and told her that I needed to smoke or have sex, and she told me no."

He didn't say anything to me, but he was giving me an intense stare. Ryder seemed like a good dude, so I was sure the answer to this question would be no.

"Can we have sex, please? I need it," I begged.

He shook his head, but his eyes never left mine as I felt them welling up with tears.

"No, Pilar, you *think* you need it. I have a list of things that you can do for coping..."

"NO!" I screamed, interrupting him.

His eyes squinted like he was getting ready to curse me out, but I was ready.

"You had better be lucky that people can't hear what goes on in this damn office because I would have choked the fuck out of you," he snapped.

Rolling my eyes, I replied, "Don't threaten me with a good time."

"Look, baby girl, I ain't finna nut on another nigga's seeds. I'm not a dog ass nigga like that. I'm not fucking you until I know that you are mine and after you drop those twins, baby girl."

I sat there with a pouty face while he continued to chew me out. Somewhere after he said I was still in love with my baby daddy, I stopped listening and wondered how long would it be before I fell out of love with him. If I ever did.

"Pilar, you not even listening to me," Ryder said, bringing me back into the conversation.

"I was listening to you, seriously."

"What I say?"

"You're not having sex with me until I have the twins."

"Yeah, that's one of the things that I said. Come here. I'll give you what you want…not the way you want it, but I'll give it to you."

I walked around his desk, and he rolled his chair back, inviting me onto his lap. I straddled his lap and tried to kiss him, but he dodged my kiss.

"Lean back and close your eyes," he instructed.

Following his instructions, I leaned back until my back was touching his desk. He started rubbing his fingers through my hair, massaging my scalp. That instantly made me close my eyes.

"Pilar, imagine me kissing and biting all over your neck. With every spot I bite, I place a small kiss in that...very...same...spot. I kiss all the way down to your stomach and circle my tongue in your belly button. I place a slow trail of very wet kisses until I get to your juicy ass pussy. Your clit is poking out, waiting for me to nibble on it."

"Mmmmmm."

"You like that, baby? You like the way it feels when I nibble on your clit?" he groaned.

"Yessss, more... please... more."

"Your pussy is so wet, baby! You are wetting my fingers up, mama. I can feel you grabbing on my fingers. I want you to cum, baby!"

"Rydderrr, baby, I feel you inside of me," I moaned.

"If you feel me...then cum... cum for me. This what you need, right? Cum!"

"Ahhh, oh my Gooodd,"

"That's it. Give it to me. I need it too, boo."

I shuddered as the juices flowed out of me like a faucet. My eyes opened, and I stared into his face.

"How you feel?" he asked.

"Sticky." I chuckled. "That is one of the best feelings I've had in a while. What did you do?"

"Well, for women, your scalp is an erogenous zone, and I stimulated it. While stimulating it, I talked nasty to you, and you imagined it."

"Wow! It felt so real."

"I know. That's all you get from me until we get serious, and you have the twins. I would also like to have a decent relationship with their father as well because I refuse to be in a relationship where I have to keep fighting with their father because he still loves your sexy ass."

"Yeah, you're absolutely right," I said as I got off his lap.

"It's a bathroom right there if you want to go in there and clean up."

I walked into his bathroom and looked in the mirror.

"What are you doing, Pilar?" I whispered to myself.

After everything Ryder said, I thought about Duke and wondered could that irrational ass nigga and I co-parent, ever. Ryder talking about being friends with that crazy ass nigga. I knew that would never happen. He would kill Ryder, literally. I thought about what Savannah said, and she was right. I really would hurt Ryder because I'm not over Duke. After I finished cleaning up, I walked back out into his office and told him that I needed to go. We hugged, and I promised that I would call him soon.

My phone rang as soon as I walked out his office, and it was Demarkus. I rolled my eyes because I had been avoiding his phone calls ever since my first meeting with Savannah. I figured I would answer the phone for the last time.

"Hello," I answered the phone.

"Damn, Pilar, you acting real funny with a nigga. What the fuck I do to you? You got a new nigga or something. Cap told me you were pregnant. When were you going to tell me?"

"Tell *you* what and *for* what?" I asked, and if we were face to face, he would see the very confused look on my face.

"That you were pregnant with my fucking kid."

I laughed out loud by accident. This nigga thought that I was pregnant by him.

"Look, Demarkus, I'm not pregnant by you. I'm sorry you were misinformed. We must talk in person. I'll meet you around nine at the place I smacked you and your wife up," I said and hung up the phone.

I hope that this meeting with Demarkus went over well because I would hate for him to be on my shit list, because we did start off as friends.

DEMARKUS

*P*arked across the street, I watched her bounce her ass out of Ryder's office like she was on top of the world. I was pissed because I knew she wasn't talking to that mothafuckin' lawyer about her case because she ain't got one. That silly ass reporter dropped her fucking case against her, so there is no reason that she should be seeing Ryder's stupid ass. Ryder and I went to high school together, and we pretty much met on campus. It was like that nigga was always in competition with me, and now he trying to steal my damn girl from me. I mean, she's not really my girl right now, but she is going to be, and he needs to back the fuck off. Pilar told me that we were going to meet at Olive Garden, so we could talk. I hoped that she ain't trying to break things off with me because that was not going to happen. I mean, and especially with her being pregnant with my babies, and shit. Cap told me that she was pregnant with twins, but he didn't know how far along she was.

After I watched Pilar pull off, I made my way into Ryder's building. As soon as I walked in the building, Ryder was walking out of his office.

"Money Mark, I wasn't expecting you, but I got a few minutes to spare. We can step back in my office."

"Got a few minutes to spare," I mumbled under my breath. Who the fuck this nigga think he is?

He sat his briefcase down on his desk, offered me a seat, and sat in his seat. I continued to stand while glaring at him.

"Oh, by the look on your face, this doesn't seem like this is a social visit. How can I help you?" He leaned back in his seat with his arms folded across his chest.

"Let me cut right to the chase. You need to stop fucking with Pilar," I commanded.

"Why are you using such colorful language in my office? Why do I need to stop messing with Pilar? What did she do to me?" he asked nonchalantly.

"That's my girl, and you need to leave her the fuck alone."

"That's your girl, and I need to leave her the fuck alone," he repeated.

"Nigga, are you a fucking parrot or something? You heard what the fuck I said," I spat before I turned to leave.

As soon as I put my hand on the doorknob, he spoke again, damn near setting me off.

"What if I don't?" he said from behind me.

"What if you don't?" I turned around and looked at him.

"Nigga, are you fucking a parrot or something?" he laughed, using the same line I used earlier on me.

"Ryder..."

"Demarkus. Let's not make this more than what it is. You're married, so any chance you have with her is going to be non-existent.

This will not be a competition."

"Oh, please. Everything between us has always been a competition. Every time I break a high school record, you have to come back, and break my record, in any sport. Ryder, you have been hating on me since the fucking start."

"It's not my fault that I'm better, my nigga. This conversation is over. You're dismissed."

"Heed my mothafuckin' warning, my nigga. Stay the fuck away from Pilar," I snapped and headed to the door.

"Ain't no warning. We'll see, my nigga. It'll be just like high school allll overrrr again." He chuckled as I slammed his door.

I ain't want to think about high school. That nigga fucked my girl and sent me a video of it. I couldn't lie. I was doing some fuck shit, trying to dirty mack on him with some bitch, and she ended up telling him. He ain't even say shit to me about it. He kept fucking with me like shit was cool, and a week later, he sent me a video of him fucking MY girl while MY girl had her head between the legs of the girl that I was talking shit about him to. I was pissed. He brought the camera up to his face talking about 'Don't ever try to dirty mack me again.' We didn't talk until the day we graduated high school, and that was by accident. Jacksonville is very big but very small at the same time. Since we both have elite status in the city, we run in the same circles, so we have been cordial, but when it comes to Pilar, all bets were off.

Later that night...

I'm a man of punctuality, so I was sitting in the restaurant ten minutes before nine waiting on Pilar. I made sure to get a good table in the back, so we could talk privately. I ordered us both a glass of water. The waiter had just brought our glasses of water when Pilar came in and sat across from me. The waiter tried to hand her a menu, but she turned it down, surprising me.

"Don't you think you need to feed my twins, Pilar?" I asked her.

She started laughing like something I said was funny, but it wasn't.

"Demarkus, look at me." She stood and pulled her t-shirt to back, showing off her baby bump. "We fucked last month. I am almost out of my first trimester. These are not your twins."

"So, you was fucking me while you was pregnant with another nigga's twins? What the fuck is wrong with you. Does he know?" I asked cocking my head to the side?

"That is none of your business, Demarkus," she replied coolly.

"Well whatever, they are going to be my step-kids." I laughed, but I was serious.

"That's what I want to talk to you about, Demarkus. We can't..." she started.

"No, don't tell me that," I cut her off.

"Demarkus, you and I both know what we did was wrong. I was in a vulnerable state when I fucked you, and that was just what I needed at the moment. I know you want us to be friends, but we both know that can't happen. We have already gone extremely far, and our friendship is really built on so many lies. Demarkus, I'm sorry. I honestly liked you better as Charlie."

"Pilar, I can go back to Charlie." I grabbed her hands, and she snatched them back from me.

"Things will never go back to being the same way. It's obvious that you want more with me, but I'm still in love with the twins' father. Besides, even if I was feeling you that way, you are married, and I don't break up happy homes, and..."

"Bullshit! That's an excuse, and you know it. You think all those niggas you let beat didn't have a girlfriend or a wife at home. Don't be foolish."

"I can't believe you are trying to throw my past in my face, Demarkus. You better keep it cute. Those niggas in my past were only a quick fuck so I could get some fucking money. That's it. Never had sex with them more than one time. Hell, never even talked to them again, so in no way, shape, form, or fashion, can you *ever* say that what we had going was the same. I didn't know shit about them, and they didn't know shit about me, but you knew everything about me. I didn't know anything about you, and clearly, that's obvious. I came here so we could end things amicably, but that doesn't seem like that's going to happen. So, I'll go," she snapped on me.

She tried to get up, but I latched on to her hands tightly, making her sit back in her seat.

"You think you finna make a new life with Ryder, don't you?"

"What I do is none of your damn business? Please stop acting like this before I make a scene in here. You know you ain't no stranger to these hands, Demarkus, and how you think it's going to look if you put your hands on me. Please just let me go," she said and tried to get up again.

I grabbed on to her, sitting her down one more time. I pulled my phone out of my pocket. I didn't want to have to do this to her, but she was forcing my hand. She wasn't going to fuck me as good as she did and think that she was going to fucking leave me alone. That ain't happening. I went into that 'special' folder and pulled up that one video that I watched that I kept just in case a moment like this happened. I pressed play and showed her the phone.

"Girl, it's some detectives here to see you. What happened?"

"Don't fuck me on this, Pilar?"

"Now, one could only guess what you guys were talking about. I could easily slip this in the tip mailbox. So, this shit will be over when I say it's over."

"Nigga, that little ass tape doesn't scare me. First of all, just because the way my life is going right now doesn't mirror my educated side, and it doesn't mean that I forgot what I learned in those stupid ass extra-curricular criminal justice classes. Second, you couldn't use that in court because that was obtained illegally," she seethed.

"This one is my favorite right here." I showed her the video of Duke fucking the shit out of her against the wall.

"You fucking perv, you still can't use that in court, bitch," she snapped.

"Well, a wise man once said, 'It ain't what you know. It's what you can prove in court'," I recited Denzel Washington's line from *Training Day*.

I got up and left her there at the table. Everything she said was correct. There was no way that I could use that in court because the information was obtained illegally, but a smooth tip to the press would have his ass arrested. Applying pressure would make his ass crack, but now that I think about it, if applying pressure to Pilar's pipes didn't make them burst, then I know that nigga pipes ain't going to burst with a little pressure.

DUKE

$\mathcal{T}$he mailman had just dropped of the envelope that I had dreaded opening. We had Brielle tested to see who she really belonged to. A part of me didn't want to open it, but I had to know. I wasn't going to be taking care of a kid that wasn't mine, especially since I ain't with her dumb ass mama no more. I ain't heard a peep from that bitch since I left her ass in the hospital. I really don't know what I would do if I ever saw her again, so it's probably best that I didn't see her again. Bakari had been staying the fuck out of my way. I think he been over in another part of the house. He had been texting me every day like clockwork apologizing and shit, but I ain't text him back. I wondered if he had been talking to her ass.

I grabbed my letter opener and sliced the letter open. My heart was beating so fast I thought that it would come out of my chest. My eyes scanned the letter, and I blew a sigh of relief. I ain't got no mothafuckin' ties to that bitch. Brielle wasn't mine, but she was my niece. I guess I decided to text my brother and let him know that he is now a father.

Me: Congrats, you're a father now.

Bakari: Wow! Thanks for letting me know. Duke, I'm sorry. Please forgive me, man. Please. I realized how stupid I was. Thank you for taking care of me all those years. I lost sight of that, and I feel horrible. I hope you don't treat your niece different.

Ignoring his message, I set the phone down. I couldn't wait to go rub this in Dutch's face. I went into the kitchen to grab me a plate of food and go down to the dungeon. On the way down to the dungeon, I grabbed me a blanket out the linen closet. When I went down there, I told the security guard watching over him to take a twenty-minute break. I pulled a chair up in front of his cage and stared at him. He was cold, shivering, and he looked like he had even lost a couple of pounds. We haven't given him any food or heat. The only thing he had on was his boxers. Our dungeon was below freezing temperatures. Coming from Egypt, we were used to temperatures being over a hundred degrees, so being hot down here wouldn't have phased him one bit. I wrapped my blanket around me and started eating.

"Oh, I got good news," I said in the middle of biting a big, juicy grilled steak.

I slid the letter between the bars of the cage, and let it fall to the floor. He was so cold that he didn't bend to open it. I was sure that if he would have bent down, his ass would have snapped his bones in half.

"How...long...how long I been down here?" he stuttered.

"About a week, I think. I don't know. I wasn't even counting. I don't want you to die just yet. So, you'll get a meal soon."

"Son, can I get just two minutes with that small heater? Please, just two?"

"What the fuck you just call me?" I growled.

"Son..."

"Don't you ever call me that shit ever again, my nigga. I ain't your mothafuckin' son. I wish I could change my mothafuckin' name," I snapped. "That shit just ruined my appetite." I got up, threw the whole plate away, and watched him squirm at the fact that I just wasted a big ass steak. I headed out the door before he started speaking again.

"What about…what about… the heater. Just two minutes, please. Please. Please. I'm dying."

"Just…two…minutes. Is that how Pilar begged when you were raping her, huh? Fuck outta here! You ain't getting shit! You'll get a meal in a couple of days. Be grateful for that."

I turned and walked out the dungeon, leaving him screaming my name. I had to go get on the jet right this moment if I wanted to get a few hours of sleep before I went to Pilar's appointment. She really hadn't been including me on this damn pregnancy at all. I'd texted her and asked her what she needed and when was the appointment, and she would never text me back. At first, I thought she had me on the block list until I called, and she answered the phone. I asked why she didn't text me back, and she chewed me out for asking about my kids. She said that I was stupid for asking what they needed when they weren't even born yet. This girl was going to get her ass beat if she kept fucking with me.

When the jet landed, Mariah and I went to my house, while my brothers went to my place of business. I stepped into my door and went into the kitchen to grab something to drink when I noticed that containers were left on my counter.

"Damn, Mariah, you ain't clean up before we left?" I snapped.

"Uh, yes the hell I did. Do not curse at me."

I pulled my gun from the small of my back because I know I ain't leave shit out, and I know a mothafucka ain't trying to squat in my damn house, especially when I ain't been gone but a couple weeks. The security guard that's at the front of the house doesn't work when we aren't at home because it doesn't make sense for him to be here when we are not. I started checking the rooms, looking under beds and shit. There was no sign of nobody. When I finally got to the last room, I heard the TV going. I was getting ready to bust a cap in someone's ass. I pushed the door open, and with the light from the TV and the small lamp across the room, I saw the mother of my twins laying on top of the covers naked as usual. Her hair was pulled into a tight bun on top of her head, which meant that she had washed her hair, getting my damn pillowcases wet.

Walking to the other side of the bed, I sat in front of her ankles. I started rubbing on her thighs. It wasn't on no fuck shit, but I just wanted to touch her. I hadn't touched her like this since a month or so ago. Damn, her stomach was turning into a small basketball. She barely had any stomach when I first met her, so i guess that's why she is smaller than a normal pregnancy. I started rubbing on her stomach, and her stomach was hard as hell. She sleeps so hard that she probably didn't even feel me touching her. I was making circular motions with my finger around her stomach as her chest rose and fell.

"Duke," I heard her whisper. Her eyes were still closed.

"Yes, baby, it's me. What are you doing here? I mean…not that you can't come here. This is your house too, but why are you here now?"

"Um, I just don't want to go home. I wanted to be here."

"Pilar, here is what we not about to do. You ain't about to lie to me no more."

"No more?" she questioned, and those eyes popped right open.

"Nah, you know what I mean. I'm saying, don't lie to me."

She took a deep breath and tried to sit up. She struggled a little bit, so I pulled her up by her arm.

"Girl, you ain't even big enough to be needing help like this. Girl, wait until you get bigger," I chuckled.

"Um, Demarkus has videos of us, me, you, and Swan, talking about the murder of Brandon. He told me that he would send that to the courts. Um, he has a video of us...fucking. It was in my house. I don't know..."

I held my hand up to stop her from talking. She wasn't telling me everything.

"Pilar, make it make sense. Don't leave shit out, because that's what you're doing. You're leaving shit out, and this can't work if you're lying to me."

"Okay, Demarkus is Charlie. Turns out...that nigga was fraud and was watching me for my grandfather. Apparently, Captain Robert Green is Cisco's dad. I was...was with someone at Olive Garden and saw him and his very pregnant wife walk in. I beat both of their asses and left the restaurant. When I made it home, that is when your people grabbed me. Fast forward, he called me as I was leaving a lawyer's office and told me that I had been dodging him because I hadn't talked to him in weeks since my therapist..."

"Therapist?"

"...told me that our friendship could not work out. I met with him at a restaurant after that phone call and told him that, and that's when he started talking crazy, and then showed me that video of us talking about Brandon's death and a video of us fucking right after you... you know...the debacle. I told him he couldn't use that in court because it was obtained illegally, and he had the nerve to tell me it ain't what I know, it's what I can prove in court. So, since I now know there are camera's in my house, I don't want to go back," she sputtered out.

She had my brain spent because I always knew it was something strange about that fucking Charlie dude. She still had a lot of holes in that story, but I knew she gave me the gist of what happened. I rubbed my temples because I was trying to figure out how I was going to deal with that nigga.

"Why you ain't told me nothing? You know you don't have to go through shit alone."

As soon as I said it, I automatically wanted to retract the statement, because I let her go through those rapes alone. I placed my hand on her thigh. She looked at it, and I went to move it, but she put her hand on my hand. I stared at her, trying to gauge what she was feeling, but she immediately answered, when she moved my hand around to her pussy. The heat that was radiating off of it, instantly made my dick rise.

"Duke is everything okay?" Mariah asked, walking into the room but immediately walked out, when she saw the intense stare down happening between me and Pilar. Her eyes were so intoxicating. She guided my hand up and down her pussy, and it was already wet. I slowly got on my knees by the bed, grabbed her by her thigh, and pulled her to me. My adrenaline was rushing because I was about to get a whiff of my drug that I haven't had in what felt like a long time. I wanted to take my time eating this… I needed to take my time eating this.

Placing a few small kisses up and down her lips, she was already moaning. I used my thick ass tongue to spread her pussy lips while I licked up and down it. I nibbled on them, and I could tell that was getting agitated because I wasn't where she wanted me to be. She wanted me on her swollen clit. She kept trying to guide me to her clit, but I wasn't going there yet. I didn't want her to just cum…I wanted her to have the biggest orgasm. Just so she can remember who the fuck I am. I pulled her off the bed a little more so I could get to her ass. I bit her on both ass cheeks and sucked hard, knowing that it was going to leave a hickey on them. While I was making circles around her asshole with my very wet tongue, she screamed out in so much pleasure. I came back up, and I could tell that she was ready for me to make her cum because her clit was even more swollen than before. I ran the tip of my tongue over her clit, and she jumped up. I had to lay her back down. Sucking on her clit, I stuck two fingers inside of her to tap on that G-spot. Pilar's body started bucking, and I already knew what was about to happen. She had a really big orgasm, and she was squirting too. I was happy that she still loved me enough to relax with me.

Her body was limp when I was done with her. I stood up and dropped my pants. I pulled my dick out between the hole in my boxers and tapped on her clit. I ain't never fucked her like this, but I wanted to savor the smell that would be on my boxers from all her juices. I slid inside of her, and it was like I could feel my soul leaving my body the moment I had my dick inside of her.

Unable to properly express myself by using words, I bit my bottom lip as I pumped in and out of her slowly. I should have never looked down because to see her creaming up my dick, made me harder. Under me, she whimpered, but this was different. I looked up to see her crying. I was used her crying during sex, but this was a different cry. I could have been a bitch ass nigga and kept going, but nah. Something was wrong. I pulled my dick out of her and laid on the side her face was turned.

"Baby girl, what's wrong?" I asked as I wiped her tears away that were falling down her face.

"I'm in love with you," she cried harder. "I don't want to be in love with you anymore."

I wasn't prepared for that, and that shit hit me like a ton of bricks. I took a deep breath before I started talking again.

"Can…can I ask why?" I whispered.

"Everything is different now. You were supposed to protect me, but you didn't. You were supposed to believe me, but you didn't. I'm hurt beyond repair right now, and I just can't see myself being with you anymore, plus you're married. After everything… everything I been through, you go off and marry her all because you thought I was lying. You can't even understand how hurt I am behind that. That made me look at you so different."

My face was steaming from the pain I caused her. I laid on my back, and clasped my hands behind my head, while she stared at me, waiting for me to say something.

"Boo, I am so sorry for what my brother and Dutch did to you. You can best believe that Dutch is paying for it right now. I was going to talk to you about what you wanted me to do with Bakari since I told him that I wouldn't fuck with him until I talked to you about it, but we can talk about all of that later."

I took another deep breath before I said this next thing. This was definitely going to hurt me as much as it hurt her because I was still in love with her, but if Dutch's stupid ass hadn't taught me shit else, he taught me to take responsibilities for my actions.

"Pilar, I'm pissed... extremely pissed that you don't want to love me anymore, and I can't say that I blame you. I was a horrible ass nigga to you. The one man that you gave your heart to, fucked you over after promising so many times that I would never do that to you. I'm sorry, and I will spend eternity apologizing to you. I hate myself for not believing you when it came to Dutch and Bakari's shit. I'm hurting behind this. A part of me wants to beg you, but it seems like your mind is made up. All I ask is that you let me be in my kids' life as much as I want with no paperwork from them white people or shit like that. I'll be the best father that I can be. I promise you that I am still very much in love with you, and whenever you want to work shit out, I'll be here. This is the hardest thing that I have ever had to do in my life, damn! I love you, aight?"

She nodded her head, and I leaned over and kissed her forehead. I pretended not to see her poke her lips out for me to give her a kiss on the lips.

"You want to get under the cover?" I asked.

"No, I'm fine. Are you sleeping with me?"

"Nah, I'mma go sleep in my room. Get some rest."

She looked sad. I wasn't about to play these games with Pilar. If she didn't want to be with me anymore, then that's just what the fuck it was going to be. Well, she didn't want to love me, and I ain't trying to make it hard for her. If she wants to be friends, then we can do that, but that sleeping in the bed together ain't gon' fly because she knows I'm going to want to fuck.

"Duke, please stay. Just rub on my stomach. I'll put some clothes on. Just please, I don't want to be alone."

"Aight, let me jump in the shower right quick."

I left the room she was sleeping in and went to my room. I jumped in the shower and scrubbed my body quickly. When I got out the shower, I pulled on some of my pajama pants and walked right back to Pilar's room. When I made it back, she had gotten under the covers. I swear it was like she only slept under the cover when she slept with me. I slid in the bed behind her, and once I found a comfortable spot, I started rubbing her stomach. She let out little moans every now and then, while she kissed and smelled on my forearm. Every time I showered, she smelled and kissed all over my forearm. Pilar is weird as fuck.

"Thank you for doing this for me," she whispered.

"When it comes to my kids, I will do anything."

She didn't reply as I continued to rub her stomach. She eventually fell asleep as did I.

The next morning...

My eyes popped open, and Pilar was bouncing on my dick. All I saw was her ass clapping on my dick, and all I could do was moan. Last night, she didn't want to love me any more, and this morning, she was riding my dick like a fucking cowgirl.

"Fuccckkkk, this feels so goooodd," Pilar moaned.

I ain't do shit but latch onto her waist and start fucking her back. Her pussy was soooo wet. This pregnant pussy can get fucked every day. Damn! She bounced harder and faster. I was scared that I was hurting the kids.

"Baby, this not... not hurting the kids?" I grunted while asking.

"Shhuuuttt uppp," she moaned, leaned forward off of my dick, and she squirted so hard that her liquids shot up my chest.

She got up and went to the bathroom without even looking at me. See, this wasn't what she was about to do. She wasn't going to be using me for dick. I heard the shower going, and I went to my room to get cleaned up. After I got cleaned up, I went down into the kitchen where Mariah had my breakfast ready. She had a different plate for Pilar. Moments later, Pilar came downstairs and walked right through the kitchen, only spoke to me, and kept going.

"Get yo' mothafuckin' ass back here," I growled at her.

"Duke," Mariah whispered and grabbed my wrist, but I snatched away from her.

"PILAR! DON'T MAKE ME REPEAT MY MOTHAFUCKIN' SELF."

She came and leaned against the doorway with her arms across her belly.

"Look, if you are going to be living here, then you will get along with Mariah. I don't give a damn about how you feel about her, but you will get along with her. She is still your friend."

She sucked her teeth and rolled her eyes to the ceiling.

"Roll yo' mothafuckin' eyes again. Mariah's loyalty has always and WILL always be with me. We have been friends since the damn sandbox days. You think Swan would tell me some shit about you? Hell naw, she wouldn't."

"She told you I was having an abortion." She stomped her foot with an attitude.

"You don't know who told me what. All I know is that you better be nice to Mariah while we are all living under the same roof. Do I make myself clear?" I spoke, and she rolled her eyes again.

I walked over and stood over her. Taking my index finger, I lifted her chin up to me.

"Do...I...make...my...self...clear?" I growled through gritted teeth.

"Whatever." She waved me off and went sat at the table.

She started eating quickly, and then she slowly stopped. She kept clearing her throat and pushed her plate back away from her.

"Duke, do you eat eggs?" she asked.

"No, I don't! Why?"

"Thought so."

She got up from the table, ran over to the garbage can, and puked her guts out. I got up to give her a glass of water.

"Your kids hate whatever you don't eat, and it's unfair. I try to eat Popeye's, and they throw it up before I can even finish my damn chicken leg. So, now I have to eat healthy shit. That's not fair at all," she whined.

"Pilar, I can make you some healthy fried chicken if you like. Anything you want, I can make it healthy for you," Mariah said to her.

I squinted my eyes at her, letting her know that she better not say shit smart.

"Thank you so much, Mariah. Could you get some french fries, mozzarella sticks, fried shrimp, chicken nuggets, pizza, pork chops..."

"We don't eat pork," I interjected.

"Anything fried that you can get. Please cook it for me. Thanks." Pilar kept talking like she didn't even hear me.

"Mariah, we are off to her appointment. If you need anything, just hit my hip."

As I watched her little ass bounce out of the house, I thought about how happy I was that I was having kids with the woman I loved... the woman I was in love with.

PILAR

*T*hese damn twins really had my sex drive on ten. It's like I can have sex every day, and that was the reason I was bouncing on Duke's dick as soon as I felt that morning wood poking against my ass. Was that rape? He didn't move when he woke up, so nah, it ain't. I know last night I told him that I wanted to stop loving him, and that was true, but I needed dick. Who else to get dick from other than my baby daddy?

The ride to the doctor's office was quiet until I asked him about his baby.

"It ain't no baby. It's Bakari's," he said calmly.

"Oh, so that's why you bashed his head in on camera? That was something to see."

"Hell nah, I did that because Edwina had you put in jail because Bakari was pillow talking to her about him knocking off Brandon. I thought about something she said the night of our wedding, and that made me realize that it was her who had you arrested."

My eyes were bucked, and I could immediately feel myself getting pissed the fuck off.

"I'mma kill that bitch!"

"Man, I'm way ahead of you, except I don't know where she is, and I frankly don't give a damn. My divorce will be final in about thirty days. Crazy, huh?"

"Damn! Your marriage was quicker than Kim Kardashian and Kris Humphries." I chuckled. "It's crazy how much shit has happened since we ain't talked. You know when I was in jail, I met my grandfather, Robert? It turns out that my grandfather fucked his wife's twin, which was my grandma. I met her, and it didn't go so well, so I had to curse her ass out. You know how I do. You gotta give respect to get it. At least I found out how the hell I was having twins, because I was confused as hell as to how I was having twins since I didn't know a pair of twins in the little family that I do know."

"Not exactly," he said.

I wondered what that meant, and he told me that Dutch wasn't his daddy, but his twin, Dame, was. Shocking wasn't the word when he told me that Dutch killed Dame because he was jealous, and shit, which sounded much like his and Bakari situation. His grandfather having Dutch locked in a damn ice cold dungeon had me laughing like a mothafucka. I could admit that laughing and talking with Duke felt like old times.

"Wait one damn minute. You legit ass wifed a fucking a hoe. She was fucking your dad, you, and your brother. Damn! She needs to kill herself."

"Sure the fuck do, before I do."

"Well, I can play devil's advocate. That Ramses' dick is something else. Maybe she wanted to try them all. You sure she ain't fucked Baron and Bomani."

"Nah, they loyal to me. So, why you seeing a therapist? Don't look at me like that. I let you slide last night because you was crying and shit, but what's up?"

"Duke, I just need to learn how to process my feelings. You know I drown my feelings in weed and sex. I'm sorry for jumping on you this morning, but I needed to relieve this pressure. I won't do it again. I don't want to send you mixed signals."

"Whatever, P."

We pulled up to the doctor's office, went inside, and checked in. I was so thankful that it wasn't packed inside. I was immediately called to the back. After the nurse got my vital signs, I jumped on the bed and waited for Dr. Keys's sexy ass to come in. Duke's ass had been quiet ever since I said something about sending him mixed signals.

"Duke, why are you being mean to me?" I asked trying to cut the tension in the room.

"I ain't being mean. It's just that I don't want to be on this emotional roller coaster with you, Pilar. If you ain't gon' fuck with me, then don't be all on my dick. Let's just co-parent and shit. Do what we have to do for the twins, and that's it."

"You don't have to be so fucking hostile about it. This is all your fucking fault to fucking begin with," I spoke louder than I meant to.

"Who the fuck you yellin' at up in here because..."

"Pilar, I thought we were working on that stress," Dr. Keys said, walking in the room, not acknowledging Duke just yet.

I guess we had gotten pretty loud, and he could hear us outside the door. He was smelling so good like always.

"I have been working on it. I went to go see Savannah, and she has been helping me get my life together."

"That is great! I'm so happy for you! So, how are you doing? How are the twins doing? Any throwing up?"

"Yes, it seems like my kids don't like nothing that their dad likes. It's unfair because they hadn't even been born yet, nor met their father. It's so frustrating. I can't even enjoy a box of Popeye's chicken."

I cut my eyes at Duke, and he was looking at me like he wanted to hit me upside my head. I could have introduced him to Duke, but since he wanted to act stupid, then I was going to act stupid as well. Black ass. Sexy ass. Ugh, I hated him.

"Well, good because you don't need to be eating a box of fried chicken. It's not good for the children."

"See, what you not going to do is act like I'm not here. Pilar, stop fucking playing with me for real. I don't know when you got this lil' childish streak in you, but you are definitely not the girl that I used to know or the girl that I fell in love with. You starting to piss me off," Duke snapped on me.

"I became a different woman when I was handcuffed to a fucking bed getting raped and pissed on. I was even more different when the man that I fell in love with cut me off and married a hoe because he didn't believe that his uncle was a rapist," I snapped back.

Damn! I shouldn't have said that! Fuck!

As he was nodding his head up and down, his eyes glossed over. I swear that I felt like a piece of shit for saying that. I could tell that he was blinking back tears. Hell, both of our lives was fucked up, and it's like the only peace that both of us could get was with each other, and I was sure that I just fucked that up.

"Um, maybe both of you..." Dr. Keys started.

Duke held his hand up, stopping him from talking.

"Just rub the cold shit on her stomach and print out the picture so we can go. I don't want to hear anything else," Duke ordered.

Dr. Keys did exactly what Duke told him to do and didn't say another word. I looked at him as he stared at the screen. Moments later, the babies' heartbeats came alive in the room.

"Baby number one is right here, and baby number two is right here. At your next appointment, we will be able to tell you what you are having," Dr. Keys spoke.

"Duke...baby, these are our kids," I whispered to him, but he didn't even look at me.

I tried to grab his hand, but he snatched it away from me.

"Is there a list of things that she doesn't need to be doing, eating, or any of that shit?" Duke asked Dr. Keys.

"Yes, there is. I can get you a list if you give me one moment. I'm going to print this out for you guys, and then get you that list, Mr. Ramses."

"I ain't tell you my name, Doc. How much do y'all be talking about me?"

"Not much. I attend your little club sometimes. I recognize you from the pictures," he replied.

"My *little* club?"

"My apologies, I didn't mean it like that. It's really a pleasure to meet you. When she did tell me about, Duke, I didn't think it was you." He held his hand out for Duke to shake, but he just looked at it.

I pray my kids aren't as mean as their stupid ass daddy, I thought to myself.

Dr. Keys handed me pictures of the ultrasound and told me to set up my next appointment on my way out the door.

In the car, Duke still had a pissy ass attitude. I had set up an emergency appointment with Savannah, so I put the address in his GPS system so he could drop me off.

"What are you doing for the rest of the day?" I asked, trying to make conversation.

"Getting them damn cameras and shit out of your house and getting more information on that Demarkus dude so your ugly ass can be safe. Get out of my car, and I'll have Mariah come get you," he said.

As soon as I got out of his car, he sped off damn near kicking rocks on me. I rolled my eyes at the back of his car. I checked in and waited for Savannah to call me to the back. It was a ten-minute wait because she was still with her client.

"Pilar," she called me, and I followed her to the back.

As soon as she got behind her desk, I started talking. She couldn't even get her pencil to the paper before I started telling her about the events that took place at the dinner with Robert then talked about Ryder, Demarkus, and Duke.

"Wow! I can see you were a busy little bee yesterday. Where do you want me to start?"

"You the professional? What you mean?"

"Well, first, what did I tell you to do when you feel yourself getting angry? You snapped for no reason. There is no reason that you should have reacted that way. What did you expect Mrs. Green to say when her husband of decades tell her that he had an affair with her twin sister, conceived a child, and now have a new grandchild?"

"Savannah, you didn't hear how she was saying it. She was saying it in such a mean way, and I didn't appreciate it. So, I had to get her together and let her know who the hell I was. She didn't even know my name, and she was calling me homeless, and some type of charity case."

"I understand where you are coming from. Everything doesn't need a response, regardless because guess what? She's going to say what she wants to say anyway. Then you told her that she trapped her husband, Pilar, you were way out of line, and I think you should apologize."

"No, she's going to think I want something from her, and that is so far from the truth."

"Okay, let's come back to that conversation because we are not going to get anywhere with that one? So, do you plan on reporting Demarkus to the proper authorities."

I shook my head no because I knew that Duke was going to take care of it. Also, I couldn't tell on his ass because he has those tapes, and it ain't no telling what he else he got on them tapes.

"Is there a reason why you're not going to tell your grandfather about his squad leader?"

"No," I simply replied.

"There is always a reason. You don't have to tell me right now, but does this reason have anything to do with your children's father? Does he plan on handling him in some type of way? I don't want to see you get in trouble, Pilar. Do you understand me?"

I nodded my head and prayed that she went on to another conversation. After a few moments of not saying anything, that is exactly what she did.

"Pilar, leave Ryder alone until you are fully over Duke." She started a new topic. "Ryder appears to be a very decent guy."

"Look, Savannah, I'll never be over Duke. He is my kids' father, and I will have to see him, every day. I'll have to look into these two beautiful faces every day that will be the spitting images of their father. If you don't know, their genes are very strong."

"I don't think you want to be over Duke. I think you want to still have him while you try to figure yourself out. Seriously, Pilar, don't ruin Ryder for the next woman because when the time comes and you choose Duke, because *you will* choose him, Ryder is going to be left in the wind, broken-hearted. That is what starts the vicious cycle of men becoming dogs."

"I'm not the highest grade of weed in the dispensary, but what I do know is no one can turn bad because of someone else. You turn bad because you want to. If a person is really a good person, then no one can change how they view someone else, and that's point blank, period."

"It seems like you got it all figured out, Pilar."

"I really don't. That is just common sense to me. Okay, next." I chuckled.

"Finally, you were wrong for broadcasting his business in front of Dr. Keys. I understand that you were angry, but what I tell you about not thinking before you speak? That tongue hurts worse than anything because you can't take those words back. Also, stop having sex with him. How do you expect to get over someone you love if you keep having sex with them?"

"Savannah, I can't have sex with no one else while I'm pregnant, so why not have sex with my baby daddy, right?"

"Wrong. You already told him that you don't want to love him anymore, so what you think he is thinking when you jump his bones in his sleep?"

"Uuugghhh, you are right!"

"I know, baby! Now, go take charge of your emotions and your attitude. We will reconvene next week, deal? I want very good news next week. Now repeat after me."

"Pilar will not have sex with anyone," she said.

I just stared at her, and then she gave me one of those big mama squints that you get when you cutting up in church, so I repeated what she said under my breath.

"Pilar will not curse anybody out."

"Look..."

"Repeat it."

"Pilar will not curse anybody out... happy?" I repeated and rolled my eyes.

"Sure am. I'm sure I have to add more to that list, but that is all I got for you right now." She smiled a very toothy smile.

Seriously, Savannah was so beautiful. She gets me all the way together, and I'm starting to love her for it. She reminded me of a thicker Lisa Raye. She better be glad that I was pregnant because I would be trying to fuck her. I knocked those thoughts to the back of my head, and smiled at her back, and left out of her office.

As soon as I walked outside, I saw the black truck waiting for me. The man got out and opened the door for me. Mariah was in the back looking at her phone.

"Hi," I spoke.

"Hello," she replied, not even looking up from her phone. "I have gotten you most of the food except for pork chops. I put your chicken and fried cheese in the oven, and it should be done by the time we get back."

"Fried cheese? Mozzarella sticks," I laughed.

"It's all the same thing, but you get it," she said and then looked at me. "Pilar, I want to talk to you about the whole shit with Edwina and Duke, but I couldn't. I really hope you understand. Duke is my best friend, but I also work for him. If I had of told you that, he would have fired me, and I need this job. I don't know if this helps, but I told him to leave you alone, honestly, because you were...or are... broken. Duke didn't need to mess you up further, and he thought he knew what he was doing, but he didn't, and you still ended up getting hurt. I always have Duke's best interest at heart, and that won't stop."

"Broken?" I asked for clarification.

"Pilar, you didn't trust men. You only used them for one thing and one thing only. You didn't open up to anybody. Duke peeled back all those layers, for him to do you the same way. Your eyes gave me the clarification that I needed that you don't trust him anymore. So, I rest my case." She sat back in her seat, and I started looking out the window.

She was right. My trust was completely broken by that. Who the fuck gets married directly after the woman he's supposedly in love with tells him she got raped? As we pulled in the gates to Ramses Avenue, I thought about what Savannah said,... *because when the time comes and you choose Duke, because you will choose him, Ryder is going to be left in the wind, broken-hearted.*

EDWINA

As soon as I touched down in Jacksonville, Florida, I got my phone turned back on, but I got a Florida number. After that, I found me a nice little loft downtown, and I loved it. I had my own space that I could call my own. I stayed close to a bank, so it was easy for me to walk there and get a bank account. I would be able to Uber around until I got a car or if I got one since Uber was so convenient to me. I also needed a bank account so I could have some of my native clothes shipped here over night.

I was so happy to be in the States. I mean, it was better than being cooped up in Egypt in the Ramses household. I can only imagine what is going on over there since I left…well not left, but got kicked out. My baby is one month now, and I miss her dearly. I have been trying to get through to Bakari, but he hadn't been picking up for me. If I had to guess, they now know that the baby belongs to Bakari. I'm even more surprised that I haven't heard from Dutch because I called his private line and left a message. As much as he told me that he loved me, you would think that he would have tried to contact me.

I had been cooped up in this loft the whole time I been here, and I decided to get out tonight. I knew that Duke had a club or something here, and it was easy as hell to find since he was so damn arrogant and named everything after his ass. My Uber called me and let me know that he was two minutes away like the app didn't already tell me that. I put on my shoes so I could meet him downstairs. I was going to the mall to get me something to wear.

As soon as I was seated in the Uber, I called Bakari. I was sure he wouldn't answer like always, but it is worth a try. The phone barely rang before he picked it up. I wasn't even prepared.

"HELLO!" he shouted into the phone.

"Ba…Bakari, hi," I whispered, "It's me."

"Who the fuck is *me*?" Bakari growled into the phone.

"Um, Edwina. How is my baby?"

"Bitch, you have some mothafuckin' nerve to even be hitting me up! It looks like you callin' from Jacksonville. Wait until I tell my brother this shit. He gon' murk your fuckin' ass."

"Bakari," I cried into the phone. "I thought you loved me. So, what we built was a lie?"

"Edwina, I wish I could give a fuck about you crying on this fuckin' phone. You were fuckin' my brother, me, and my daddy, all at the same fucking time. Seriously tho'? I ain't never heard of no shit like that in my life. I feel like we need to go on the *Jerry Springer Show*. You a fuckin' hoe, and you will never see Brielle again. Talkin' bout *what the fuck we built*. Fuck outta here," he barked and hung up.

I didn't even think you could hear someone hang up on you with an iPhone, but I swear I heard a click. I tried to call him back, and it didn't go through, so I knew that he had me blocked. I knew then that I would never see my daughter again. Well, he took something from me, then I was going to take something from him. His brother.

"Ma'am, we are here," the Uber driver said.

"Okay, great!"

I got out and went into the mall. There were so many stores full of clothes. I wasn't used to doing shit like this. I normally had people shopping for me. People were looking at me funny because of the way I was dressed, and it was hotter than hell outside, but I was used to it. I guess since I can't return to Egypt, then I will have to get some more clothes. Like they say, 'when in Rome, do as the Romans do.' I was walking through the mall, trying to figure out what style clothes I would want. I went to this store called Dillard's and started sniffing the perfumes. I looked up, and I saw Mariah, but she wasn't paying attention. I shifted by the cabinet, so they wouldn't see me.

Mariah was standing in front of that curly haired bitch. When she turned to the side, I saw her big ass belly, and I nearly fainted. Duke had gotten this bitch pregnant. I almost blew my cover because I stepped away from around the corner. She looked my way, and she squinted a little like she recognized me, but she looked back at Mariah. I walked away quickly. I needed to get out of there. I put in for an Uber to come pick me up. It said that it was ten minutes away, so I sat on the bench, and waited. While I was waiting, a fine ass man walked up and sat next to me. I normally liked dark skin men, but this yellow man was too cute to pass up. I was going to let him say something to me first. I hope he said something to me before my Uber pulled up.

"Hey, beautiful," he said with his hand out for me to shake. "My name is Fredrick, yours?"

"My name is Edwina," I smiled at him.

"Jesus Christ, your accent is beautiful. Where are you from?"

"I am from Egypt. Are you from around here? I moved here a month ago."

"Yes, born and raised. Maybe I can show you around sometime."

"Sure, I would love that. You can put your number in my phone. I live downtown." I handed him my phone so he could store his number in it.

"I can take you home if you are waiting for the bus or something."

"Nah, I'm fine. That look like my Uber pulling up right there."

He walked me over to my Uber and opened the door for me. I told him that I would call him later, and the Uber driver drove off.

"Look, I need a huge favor from you. I need you to ride around this mall until I tell you to stop. I will give you a hefty tip, please."

"Ma'am, are you trying to kill someone?" the driver asked.

"No. Absolutely not."

Not yet, I thought to myself. We only rode around the mall for at least forty-five minutes before those two bitches came out the mall with bags full of shit on both arms. She was getting helped into a black truck.

"This bitch got a driver. Hell no!" I mumbled to myself. "Follow that truck. I promise I'm not going to kill them."

Inconspicuously, we followed them for about forty minutes

before they pulled up to a large gate. I could see three houses and the top of another one.

"Oh, that's Ramses Avenue. We can't get back there," the driver said.

"Wow! Okay, you can take me home now!"

The whole ride home, I was fuming. He had this bitch over here living like she was a fucking princess and shit. I was sure this bitch barely had to bath herself. That was supposed to be me. I prayed that Bakari didn't tell Duke that I was here yet because I needed to do a sneak attack. I looked at the phone and realized that today was Duke's birthday. Everything happened so out of order. This was the original day that he was supposed to move back home, marry me, and we make a basketball team of kids. Fuck! I knew that would never happen, so I texted Fredrick and asked him if he wanted to meet me at Duke's. He texted me back and said it was cool. I was going to have this Uber driver drive me back to the mall, but I decided not to. I would put in for another one. This make-over was going to make Duke regret the fucking day that he left me.

DUKE

$\mathcal{T}$oday was a real nigga's birthday. Man, this time last year, I was excited as shit because I knew that I had one more year before I became King. This shit was so crazy because it's so funny how much time can change in one year. I truly haven't thought about that crown at all, so right now, it's still hanging in the wind, and my grandpa is sitting as King right now until I make up my mind. I couldn't wait until I celebrated my birthday at my place. You had to buy tickets to get in, and it was crazy how fast the place sold out.

"Happy Birthdayyyy, baby! I decided to serve my king in bed this morning," she said as she backed in the room with the tray of food. She placed the tray at the end of the bed, and jumped in my lap.

"Mandee, you're really the best. You know that! Give daddy a kiss."

She cheesed like a little school girl, before she placed her lips on mine and gave me some tongue.

The day that Pilar pulled that shit in the doctor's office, I was pissed off. I hadn't seen her since that day. She'd been trying to get back on my good side, but I told her not to text me if it ain't have shit to do with the twins' appointments or any of that shit. It's been a month since

I stayed at the house with her and Mariah. I had been staying at my loft downtown. She didn't know where I was staying because she didn't know about this spot. I knew my brothers, nor Mariah would tell her about this spot, so I wasn't worried about her popping up.

Mandee Rae Blake was the most beautiful chocolate stallion that I ever met. She was thirty, six foot tall, and thick like a mothafucka. She is from Gabon, which is in Africa, but she moved over here when she was younger, so she was basically raised in the states. She taught English at one of the high schools. She loved to read, and write. She spoke English, French, and Arabic. She was amazing. Mandee was everything Pilar was not. She didn't argue with me nor did she do childish shit to piss me off. I knew it had been a month, but damn, she is making me fall fast. I met her the same day that Pilar pissed me off. She was at the gas station, filling up her Mercedes. All I could see was a sexy ass, established woman.

"Damn, baby, why you staring at me like that?" She giggled.

"You are so beautiful, and I already can't wait to get you back here tonight. I can only picture how beautiful you are going to look in that dress tonight."

"Well, my baby made sure that I match his fly. That Balmain is going to look fly on my body. Couple of questions though. Is she going to be there? I don't want any problems with her. I would like to meet her. She is very beautiful from how you described her," she said before kissing my forehead.

Mandee knew about Pilar, but I didn't tell her the other shit because she didn't need to know all of that. She just knew that I had twins on the way, and I had no dealings with their mother, only about the twins. Truth is… I miss the fuck out of my baby mama, but she had said that she didn't want to love me anymore, and I was giving her that by moving on. Was it hard? Yes. Was it easy? No. I'm in feelings now that she hadn't text me for my birthday. Fuck it!

"Nah, she's going to be home. She's almost seven months pregnant. She doesn't need to be in that crowd because if something happens to her… my kids, I would kill someone."

"You would be well within your rights if you did."

"Come give mama some of that morning wood that's damn near poking me through my panties."

She got off me and put the tray of food on the top of the dresser. She got a condom out of the night stand and slid it on my dick. Staring deep into my eyes, she slid down on my dick. The pleasure made me close my eyes. Guiding her by her waist, I slid her up and down on my dick slowly.

"Damnn! This juicy ass pussy feels good as hell. Fuck. Let daddy hit you from the back."

She crawled off me and assumed the position. I dipped into her goody box and started pounding her as if my life depended. I wished that her ass would squirt on me the way that I make Pilar's do. I could hit her in a spot so good, that'll make that pussy rain down on me like a fucking rain storm. The last time we had sex, and she stood up and squirted on my abs, and chest, I fell in love all over again. The fact that I was the first nigga to even make her do that. Fuckkk! She was going to always be my bitch.

"Duuukkkkeeee, DAMN! You beating this pussy up," Mandee screamed, bringing me back to earth. I completely blacked out for a minute.

"You gon' cum! Huh? You gon' cum! Cum for me, Mandee, fuck," I groaned.

I ripped the condom off and came on her big ass. We weren't doing oral sex yet. Everybody didn't get that. The day I don't use a condom is the day that I will eat the shit out of this fat ass pussy.

My phone rang, and I quickly grabbed it, thinking that it was Pilar, but it was Baron.

"Yeah, fool," I answered the phone.

"Bring your old ass downstairs, nigga. You need a walker or a cane or something? Old ass nigga."

"Nigga, I can still run a mile in seven minutes. What can you do?" I laughed.

"Whatever, nigga! I bet you can't beat my ass. You might need a hip replacement after I fold you up like a chicken wing." He laughed.

"Shut up, bitch! I'll be downstairs in a minute. Give me a minute," I said and hung up the phone.

"You and your brothers are so funny." She laughed.

"Yeah, I know, man. Never a day without joking," I replied.

I went into the bathroom, took care of my hygiene, jumped in the shower, and washed my body off. I jumped out and pulled on a Nike sweat suit.

"I'll be back to pick you up later, aight?" I said and placed a kiss on her cheek.

When I made it downstairs, Baron and Bomani was getting out of the truck.

"Damn, hoe, when you said a minute, I literally thought you meant putting on your shoes and coming downstairs," Baron said, dapping me up.

As soon as we got in the truck, it got quiet as a mouse, and they were both staring me upside of my head.

"WHAT" I snapped.

"You really serious about this broad, man?" Baron asked.

"I mean..."

"Hell naw, you ain't. Don't play with that girl feelings, man. She seems like she really likes you, bro. Then you making a mockery out of P by bringing her to the party, knowing that there gon' be pictures and shit all over social media," he spoke, and then tapped me upside of my head. "You bein' reckless and stupid. That girl has been worried sick about you, crying every night. You know she ain't stopped throwing up, and you over here playing house with a bitch you barely know, but it's all good, though. You got me feeling the twins moving inside of her stomach and shit because you not there. Mercy be looking at me all side-eyed when I am talking to her stomach. Basically, doing shit that you are supposed to be doing. At least they'll know the accent."

"What you mean throwing up? I thought that shit stopped after three months. Damn, they started moving in her stomach. I feel like shit now, but Mandee is a real cool girl, and she ain't shit like Pilar. Like, she be listening to everything I tell her to do. No back talk. I ain't got to argue or none of that shit."

Baron and Bomani started laughing so hard.

"Damn, bro! Even a damn dog don't listen to everything you say do. You know that's been Pilar since DAY ONE! You wildin', bro, but if you tryin' to make ol' girl your legit girl, then I'll support you," Bomani said. "P will always be my favorite because she can check your black ass like no other woman can."

I nodded my head as we headed to the Tuxedo store to pick up our suits. We were going to be so fly tonight, and I couldn't fucking wait. I planned on getting shit faced drunk to the point where my brothers got to drive me home.

Later that night...

I picked up Mandee from the loft, and she was looking gorgeous as shit. Damn, I couldn't wait to take that damn dress off her. When we pulled up to Duke's the line was wrapped around the corner. The driver pulled around to my spot and got out. As soon as we stepped inside of the club, they had three shots waiting for me. I was mingling with the crowd, and it was time for me to get on stage. I grabbed Mandee by her waist, and I walked with her on the stage. I took the mic from the DJ and started speaking.

"Y'all, I wish I could explain how happy I am that y'all decided to celebrate my birthday with me. I guess I might as well introduce y'all to my girl, Mandee. She has been holding me down for a lil' minute now. When you see her...know that this is me. I'm feeling fucking generous tonight. Two free round of drinks for everybody. Another thing..."

"You son of a bitch," a voice cut me off.

I looked into the crowd and saw Pilar, Swan, and Lee, but I wasn't sure who said that. They were parting like the red sea for them. I watched as the love of my life waddled her ass to the front with a small bag in her hand. She was in a beautiful gown that had a deep V that had her swollen breasts sitting up good. She had her hair straightened, and I could feel my dick getting hard just by thinking about wrapping my hand around it, pushing her stomach down on the bed, and fucking her from the back. Her stomach was so beautiful, and I was missing everything.

"THIS IS THE SECOND FUCKING TIME THAT YOU HAVE DONE THIS SHIT. I AM SO FUCKING SICK OF YOU. YOU WASN'T MAN ENOUGH TO DUMP MY BITCH IN PERSON. YOU A FUCKING DICK!" Swan yelled, and everybody instantly started pulling out their cell phones.

"Happy Birthday, Duke," she spoke so softly, but I could hear the defeat in her voice.

At that moment, I knew she was done. Done trying. Done trying to talk to me. Looking in her eyes, I didn't see anything. No tears. Her face was blank. She handed me the bag, and she turned to walk away. Lee was holding the train of her dress, and Bomani had latched on to her arm. She had leaned on his arm, so I knew that she was crying, and I felt like shit.

"TO THINK THAT I TOLD HER TO GIVE IT ONE MORE CHANCE. YOU DON'T KNOW HOW MANY NIGGAS WAS TRYIN' TO WIFE HER WHILE SHE PREGNANT WIT' YO' SEEDS, YOU BITCH ASS NIGGA. YOU A FUCKIN' BITCH! I HATE YOU!

EVERYTHING SHE BEEN THROUGH…WITH YOU…YOUR FAMILY…AND THIS IS HOW YOU REPAY HER. YOU A BITCH," Swan cried out in pain for her friend. Baron came and picked her up to carry her out.

"YOU A BITCH. YOU A BITCH. YOU A BITCH," she kept screaming at the top of her lungs until I couldn't hear her anymore.

Everybody was staring at me, and honestly, I didn't even know what to say after that. I gave the mic back to the DJ, and he turned the music back on. Thankfully, a local artist was in there, and he took the opportunity to jump on stage to hype the crowd back up. Mandee and I were walking off the stage until I felt somebody grab onto my arm, and it was the DJ. I told Mandee to keep walking while I talked to him for a minute.

"Bruh, I'm telling you now! Go check on your seeds, bro. It's one person in the world that you don't ever want to piss off, and that's your baby moms. They say happy wife, happy life, but it's happy baby moms, happy life. Seriously. Right now, she is the person that you are guaranteed to be tied to for the rest of your life. Who you want to piss off more?" He nodded his head toward Mandee. "Her or the girl that's carrying your seeds? Shouldn't be a hard choice. I'll holla at you later, boss," he said and walked off.

I walked over to Mandee and took her upstairs to my office. I needed to regroup. I took a shot of alcohol, and then another one. I threw the bag on my desk and flopped down in the chair.

"Baby, is everything okay?" she asked.

"Do it look like everything is alright?" I snapped.

"Baby, I'm sorry. I didn't mean to upset you. I'll leave you alone for a moment," she said and scattered out of the room.

I opened the bag that she got me. It was a small card and two boxes. The smaller box had *Blue Nile* on it, and when I opened it, it was a pair of diamond studs. I remember I was telling her about some diamond studs, but I had never ordered them. The other box had *Hublot* on it. I hurried up and opened it because I had been wanting one of these watches forever. It was a Hublot Big Bang Gold midsize watch, which ran about twenty thousand dollars. I read the note.

"Duke, I really hope you like your gifts. Don't worry, I used my own money. Well, it's money you put in my account. I don't know if it counts or not. I know you had been wanting these two items. I hope we can talk later."

I put the gifts back in the bag and called Pilar. Of course, she didn't answer, but she sent a text.

Babymama: *Twins are fine.*

Me: *I just want to talk to you. You wanted to talk. That's what your note said.*

Babymama: *Twins are fine.*

I guess she was about to play these childish ass games, and I didn't have time for it. I threw my phone down on my desk so I could get up and go find Mandee.

PILAR

$\mathcal{T}$wo times. Two times he has shown off women that weren't me. I feel like New York from Flavor of Love where Flava Flav dissed her twice. Didn't pick her the first time, brought her back for the second season, and still didn't pick her again. I am New York right now. I thought that I cried my last tear, but I guess I didn't because before I could even get in the truck good, I was bawling my eyes out. I didn't care how late it was, I texted Savannah, and told her that I need an emergency session before I lost what mind I had left. The crazy thing about this was I had been asking God for a sign, and I got the sign that I needed.

"Sis, it's going to be alright," Bomani rubbed the side of my face, as I continued to cry on his shoulder. Lari was rubbing my thigh trying to console me, and I honestly didn't know why I couldn't stop crying.

"Come on, sis. You fuckin' with me for real. Please stop crying. Take some deep breaths or something before you pass out or some shit. Think about the twins," he said.

I started to calm down a little because the twins were most important. I heard screaming, and I looked up to see Baron carrying Swan out over his shoulder. He opened the door and put her in the front seat.

"Aye, Bomani, get out. The driver is going to make sure they get home," Baron spoke.

Bomani kissed me on my forehead, and then leaned over and gave Lee a nasty ass kiss on the mouth. They shut the door, and the driver drove off.

"Pilar, it's over for Duke! Let that nigga have that bitch! Don't talk to him, if it's not about the kids. Do you understand me?" Swan commanded as she continued to wipe her tears away? "I'm so sorry, Pilar. I swear I wish there was more that I can do. You don't deserve that shit. Fuck that nigga."

I nodded my head. I instructed the driver to drop me off at my therapist's office. I was literally thankful for her. As soon as I got out the car, Duke was texting me asking can we talk because that's what my note to him said. I couldn't even believe that he texted me that shit. Nah, nigga, we only going to talk about the kids from here on out, and that's on everything I love. Nigga, had a whole other girlfriend, like was he fucking with that bitch when we were going together. Like, he was showing this bitch off like they were very comfortable with each other. I mean, I had cut off Ryder for his ass. Oh my God!

"Ms. Harrison, do you need us to wait for you, or..."

"I'll Uber home," I said to him.

"Lari, are you sure you are alright," Lee asked.

"No, I'm not alright, but I'm about to talk to my therapist now, and I'll be fine after this session," I replied.

"Pilar, I want to come in with you," Swan said.

"I'm good, baby. Y'all go to the house. I'll be there," I assured her.

I shut the door and watched them drive off. I walked slowly into the building and locked the door like she told me. I walked into her office, and she was sitting there in some jammies with a cardigan.

"Pilar, you okay? You look very beautiful and very pregnant. Your hair is even more beautiful straightened. Jesus Christ."

I offered her a weak smile, but I shook my head no. I told her about the events that took place tonight. She already knew that Duke and I weren't on speaking terms.

"Is this the reason that you missed your monthly check-up on the twins. You were supposed to find out what you were having, but you were a no-show. Don't you neglect your doctor, because if you neglect your doctor, then you are essentially neglecting your children."

"Ugh! Tell, Dr. Keys to stop telling my damn business." I chuckled. "I couldn't get out of bed. I was depressed, and I literally prayed every night that God would send me a sign, and I got it. The only conversation we are going to have now is about the kids, and that was on my dead mom and grandmother's grave. If he wants to get mad because I snapped on him about the truth, then whatever."

"Well, I told you it is a time and place for everything. You shouldn't have said that at all. Dr. Keys told me all your business because you signed a release form for us to speak."

"I cut a lawyer off for him. A lawyer that could make me cum just by talking to me, and rubbing my scalp at the same time." I laughed at how stupid I had been.

"Pilar, don't do it. You're not ready for another relationship," Savannah said, but my mind was already made up.

"Savannah, I'm over Duke," I spoke.

"Well, why are you about to cry again?"

"I'm upset. That's why."

"You're upset because you love him. Pilar, you don't just turn your feelings off with a switch, and that is okay. The more you tell yourself that you don't love him, the harder it's going to be for you to get over the situation."

"You're right! I have to go," I stated.

"Pilar, you are to upset. I can't let you leave like this."

"Savannah, I'm not a danger to myself or him or that bitch. I'm going home to get out this dress and get under the covers. Scouts honor," I said, holding up the sign with my fingers.

"Okay, call me when you get home. I swear I will send the police over to your house."

I hugged her tight. I put an Uber, and just my luck, one was two minutes away. I waited outside, and they pulled up. I was headed to the airport, with only one destination in mind. I needed answers, and there was only one person that could give them to me.

PRINCE HARRISON

$\mathcal{I}$t's funny that after my little spat with my parents a while back, they had been acting real cordial and trying to meet Pilar. If I had of known all it took was a little choke and an insight on how I got the bulk of my money, then I would have been done that shit. I had still been working around the church, preaching whenever my daddy needed me too. Don't judge me. I love the Lord, but I still needed money.

It hurt my heart to see my daughter laid up in a hospital after being raped, and then the next time I saw her, she would be knocking a damn reporter down at the jail as a suspected murderer. My parents hit me with the side eye real quick because I knew my baby wasn't any damn killer. That's why I sent my lawyer, Serena, down there to get some insight, and I was pissed that she turned her away, saying she didn't want or need my help.

At this point, I was tired of praying that my daughter came back to me. I just needed one full hour to explain to her.

"Prince, your forehead is wrinkling. Are you okay?" Karen asked as she walked out the bathroom.

Karen had been my girlfriend for a few months, and she was a wonderful woman. She was patient with me, and that's what I needed. She was the only woman that I have really opened up to besides my Coco. She knew almost everything about me.

"Nah, just worried about my daughter that's all. I want her back in my life, and I don't know what more to do."

"Well, Prince, God is an on-time God. He may not come when you want him, but he is always on time. You know that. Now, come get in the bed, and stop worrying before those wrinkles stay in your forehead, because I don't know if I can date a hotdog forehead man," she said and pulled the covers back.

"You're right, baby."

As soon as I slid under the cover, I heard a big clap of thunder, and it started pouring down raining. Rain always helped me go to sleep. I cuddled up with Karen and went to sleep.

Hours later, I woke up to Karen nudging me.

"Prince, your phone is ringing, and it won't stop. Answer it, and please get back in the bed," Karen sleepily said.

My phone had started back ringing, and I grabbed it without looking at the caller ID.

"Yeah," I answered the phone sleepily.

"Why don't you love me," a voice cried in the phone.

I pulled the phone back to look at it, and the number wasn't saved in my phone. I put the phone back to my ear. I couldn't tell the voice because of the crying.

"Prince Harrison, why didn't you love me?" she cried.

Only one person in the world calls me by my full name— my daughter. I quickly sat up in the bed. I nudged Karen for her to get up.

"Pilar, baby, what are you talking about? I have always loved you. I never stopped. I loved you since the day that you were born."

"Why were you never there for me? I had nobody in my corner. You let..."

Everything after that was very inaudible because she was crying so hard.

"Pilar, baby girl, please calm down. I can't hear you. Why does it sound like you are standing in the rain?"

"I am. I didn't know what to do. I couldn't go home. So, I came here to Jackson."

I immediately jumped up out the bed and started putting on clothes.

"Where in Jackson are you?" I asked.

"The airport."

"Pilar, get inside. I'll be right there. I'm not hanging up."

She didn't say anything, but she kept crying. Karen and I jumped in my truck and sped to the airport. This was the only time that I was thankful that I lived close to the airport. I had my Escalade on two wheels the whole way because I was driving so fast. As I got closer, I saw my very pregnant daughter with the phone to her ear, standing in the freezing cold rain, in the middle of November, with a beautiful gown on. She was asking to get Pneumonia. I barely put the car in park before I jumped out and ushered her in the truck. She had nothing but a purse, so this was a very spur of the moment trip. She laid down in the back seat of my truck. I had the heat on full blast.

"Pilar, are you crazy? You have on next to nothing, and you just standing out in the rain like a fucking crazy ass⊠"

Karen placed her hand on my thigh and shook her head.

"Baby, I'm sorry. You just have me worried, aight?" I redirected my statement.

"I know," she whispered.

I pulled into the garage. I opened the door for Karen and then opened the door for Pilar. I helped her out the truck. She was literally soaking wet. After we got in the house, I took her into the bathroom and turned the heater on. I threw a big towel on the heating rack.

"Baby, bring me a t-shirt and some shorts," I called out to Karen.

"Get undressed," I told her and turned around. "That towel should be warm by now. Wrap it around you."

"Done," she whispered.

I sat on the toilet and pulled her onto my lap. She nestled her head in the nape of my neck and started crying again. I started rocking my daughter like she was a baby.

"Pilar, I swear, I loved your mom. I still do. She is forever engraved in my heart because her name is tatted there. As you know, when you were born, they called the cops and shit because you had drugs in your system. Your mom was young when you were born, and so was I. My parents were able to get over on me. They told me that if I claimed you, it would tarnish our family name, and my dad told me that he would have me arrested. Serious shit! Pilar, I loved your mom. I hate myself so much because I feel like I could have saved her life had I just went when she called me. I told her I couldn't come until later because I was finishing shit up at the church. Oh, side bar, I'm an assistant pastor to my father...your grandfather."

I took a deep breath and continued.

"Pilar, I wanted to come around. Hell, I did, but by the time I was starting to come around, you had developed an attitude and didn't want to have any dealings with me. I would call you, but you would never answer, ever. Pilar, I was at both of your graduations. Hell, Pilar, I wrote you letters and sent you money. That was the least that I could do. Hell, when Coco was in rehab, we seriously wrote each other every day. I don't know what happened to those letters."

"I never received a letter or any money from you. I had to share food with my grandmother. I had a horrible childhood. I had to fu⊠"

"Ahhhh, don't tell me that. Please don't. Pilar. I know. I remember. They're dead," I admitted.

"Huh?"

"Every one of those nasty old men who touched you. They are floating somewhere. Pilar, I knew everything."

"You could have tried...tried harder, Prince...Harrison, but I forgive you," she whispered.

The tears of joy started falling down my eyes. I couldn't contain myself, as hard as I wanted to, I couldn't.

"Pilar," I whispered.

No Answer.

"Baby girl," I whispered again.

Nothing.

My baby girl had fallen asleep in my arms. I held her as her chest rose and fell. I picked her up and carried her to the guest room. Karen pulled the covers back, and I laid her down, covering her up. I put the t-shirt and the basketball shorts on the nightstand next to her. I pulled the chair out from the desk in the room and sat there watching her.

Hours later, I was still sitting here, staring at her as her chest rose and fell.

"Prince, come to bed. You have been watching her for hours. She's not going to leave," Karen whispered loudly at me.

"I just want to watch her. Like, I don't want to wake up, and she is gone again. I want her to wake up so we can talk."

"She will be here. I promise she will. She's not going anywhere. Come to bed, now," Karen ordered.

I kissed her on her cheek and followed Karen to the bedroom. As soon as I got undressed, I fell asleep.

The next morning...

When I woke up, Karen was out of bed. I put on my robe and went to the guest room, and I saw that Pilar's bed was made up. I ran into the kitchen where Karen was standing by the stove.

"See, I told you. I told you!" I shrieked.

"Told me what?" She turned to me with her hand on her hip.

"Good morning, Prince," Pilar came walked into the kitchen with one of Karen's robes on.

Karen rolled her eyes at me as I looked at her with apologetic eyes. She called me, Prince, so we were making progress.

"I was telling Pilar that you guys have some beautiful hair genes. I mean, this girl is very beautiful, and her hair is so long," Karen bragged on her.

"Well, it's half straight and half curly now. It'll all be curly in a few hours since my hair is still a little wet from last night."

"Pilar, how long are you going to be here?" I asked.

"I don't know. Maybe for a week. I don't know, until I'm ready to go back unless you will have me."

"You don't even have to ask me that. You know that. We can go get you some clothes, and you can hang out with me. Also, we get to eat dinner with your grandparents on Thanksgiving. Don't bend your face up. This is going to be fun," I said excitingly.

After we finished eating breakfast, I gave Pilar an extra toothbrush and stuff so she could wash her face. She told me that she wanted to take a nap, so she got in the bed. She told me her sizes so I sent Karen out to get her a bunch of clothes and shoes. I told Karen to pick out whatever she thinks Pilar would like and get her something nice as well. While Pilar napped, I napped right next to her.

Later that evening...

Pilar and I were sitting at the dinner table eating. Karen had to run some errands for her job. She was the manager at the bank. That's where I met her at.

"So, lil' mama. Are you ready to tell me why you here?"

"Long story or short?"

"I have all the time in the world for my daughter."

"Okay, it's pretty long. You're going to be mad at some parts, and you're going to squirm at some parts, but you have all the time in the world for me, so here we go."

She took a deep breath and started telling me the story.

For the next two hours, she talked non-stop, starting with Brandon all the way up until she ended up at the airport crying her eyes out. She did not lie when she said I was going to have a lot of different emotions because when she told me in detail about the rapes she endured, I wanted to travel across the country and beat those niggas ass. I also wanted to beat that nigga ass that was spitting all that hot shit at me talking about he was the one that was going to marry my daughter, and he wasn't nothing but a piece of shit and embarrassed my daughter twice. Twice. She said since Duke got rid of the cameras in the house she shares with Swan, she hasn't heard from Demarkus. She got her number changed, which is why I didn't know the number at first. Her grandfather seemed a little sketchy, but he may want a genuine relationship with her. Damn, Pilar has been through a lot of shit in just a short amount of time. I was glad that she was seeing the therapist because my baby would probably be dead by now, from stress.

"Prince, are you going to say something? Stop looking at me like that. You wanted to know, so I told you."

"How are you feeling right now?"

"I mean, it is what it is. Duke's going to be a great father, and

I would never keep the kids away from him. I would never be that woman at all. I'm not going to put him on child support because he takes really good care of me, and I know he's going to continue to do so."

"Alright then. I mean, you know I'm not hurting for money either, baby girl. If you ever need anything, you can ask me. I mean, damn! I can't wait until my grandkiddos get here. They are going to be so spoiled."

"Yes, that is true."

Pilar and I talked for the rest of the night. We talked about her childhood. I was highly pissed that Lenora never gave Pilar any of my letters. She really had my baby thinking that I didn't give a damn about her. I knew that this was the start of many very long nights. I don't know how long she was going to be here because she was going to have to go back and face her problems. What I do know is that I was going to make the best of it.

PILAR

Thanksgiving Day

$\mathcal{I}$ woke up this morning in the comforts of Prince's huge ass house. I would never have thought that he would be living like this. I have been here for the last four days, and he and I were getting to know each other. I mean, there is so much to know since we are basically like strangers to each other.

I grabbed my phone from the night stand since I hadn't touched it in four days. I had just been taking it on and off the charger so it will stay charged. I looked at my phone, and I literally had over two hundred missed calls and so many messages. I clicked my missed calls, and they were all from Duke and his brothers. Swan, Lee, and Savannah. One from Ryder. I didn't want to go in the messages, but I knew I had too. I was going to leave my read receipt on as well. I wanted them to know that I was okay. I clicked on Savannah's text thread first.

SJ: Pilar, you were supposed to call me when you made it home. What happened?

SJ: Pilar? You're scaring me. Please text me back.

SJ: Pilar, it's been days since I have heard from you. Your children's father is extremely worried about you. If you don't text me back, please let him know that you are okay.

SJ: *This is not fair for to me. I'm literally sitting here crying because I don't know if you are okay or not. I have never cried over my clients, but you are very special to me. Please let me know that you are okay. Please, I'm literally begging you.*

I was going to text her back later.

Swan: *Your therapy session been over for the last hour, where are you?*

Swan: *BITCH, THIS IS NOT FUNNY! PILAR, WHERE ARE YOU?*

Swan: *Pilar, I swear to God, you are scaring me. Where are you? I'm worried sick. Oh my God!*

Swan: *Pilar, I am crying real tears man. Please call me back. Please.*

Swan: *Duke says he sooooo sorry, and he over here pacing the floor, shaking so bad. Pilar, he's worried. We are all worried. Please let somebody know that you are safe. Come on.*

There were several more of the same messages from Swan. Lee, Baron, and Bomani were sending me the same messages. The text thread from Duke is what I was dreading reading,

Duke: *Pilar, Mariah just told me that you are not home. Where are you?*

Duke: *Stop fucking playing with me, for real.*

Duke: *Nah, for real, where you at? I know you mad at me, and I feel like shit. Where you at?*

Duke: Pilar, I'm sorry for real. Please come home. I keep fucking up, and I'm so sorry. Please forgive me.

Duke: Pilar, where the fuck you at with my kids?

Duke: I'm still in love with you, please come home, man.

Duke sent more threats and more apologies. He was the most bipolar person I ever met in my life. I was in the midst of texting Savannah back, but Bomani called, and I fucked around and answered the damn phone.

"Hello," I whispered into the phone.

"Pilar, where you at, sis!? You okay!? Man, you got everybody over here crying and shit. Talk to your bro. Where you at? Let me come get you. Nobody else, just me," Bomani rattled off.

You could tell that he had been crying. His nose sounded stopped up.

"I'm fine. Tell everyone, I'm fine."

"Sis, why you doing this to us? Come home, man. Please," Bomani cried into the phone, breaking my heart into pieces. "Pleasseee, let me come get you. It'll just be me. You got my brother over here going crazy, ma. He ain't ate or slept in days. Man, everybody is so worried."

"I have to go now. Bomani, I love you. Happy Thanksgiving," I whispered into the phone.

"Ain't no Thanksgiving without..."

I hung up the phone, and almost immediately my phone went off.

Duke: Pilar, what the fuck you say to Mani. This nigga over here wheezing and shit. He said you sound like you 'bout to fucking kill yourself. Pilar, stop fucking playing. I swear to God! Please, come home. I need you. I want to talk to my kids.

Me: *Not suicidal.*

He started calling, but I put the phone down and started getting dressed for this adventure at Prince's parent's house. I was just going to have to text Savannah later because I didn't want any more mistakenly answered phone calls. I swear, it's like I had gotten bigger since I been here. I'm just happy that I haven't thrown up since I been here. These twins were finicky.

Once I was dressed, I went into the living room where Karen and Prince were waiting for me. Karen was extremely nice. I liked her, and I could tell that he liked her a lot as well. He opened the door for us, and then he got in the truck.

"Prince, can you get me a condo and have it ready by the time I get back. I want a new car as well. If you can't..."

"Done. What kind of car do you want? I got a couple of connections in Jacksonville."

"I want something safe for the twins. Something big enough for two car seats, but no truck. Reliable. Fancy." I chuckled.

"Mercedes S550." He laughed. I saw you looking at mine. If the drive wasn't so long, I would let you take mine back. Ain't no way I'mma let you drive and you damn near due."

"You right about that."

I sat back in the seat, and moments later, we pulled into the gates of a huge house. I knew it was a reason I hated megachurch pastors. I was sure he lived lavishly, and his flock lived in the hood with broke down cars. I already knew that these mothafuckas were going to be uppity, and I will curse their asses out just like I did Lenita's ass.

"You ready to meet your grandparents?" Prince asked as he helped me out the car.

"I'm ready to meet Pastor and First Lady Harrison. By the way, what are their names?"

"Prince and Angela Harrison," Prince informed me.

"So, you a junior or the second," I asked him.

"I'm the second."

As soon as we walked up to the door, it opened. It was his parents. I knew because Prince looked just like his dad.

"Ma…Dad, you met Karen, but this is your granddaughter, Pilar Harrison. Pilar, these are your grandparents," he introduced us.

"Pastor and First Lady," I greeted them.

They invited us in, and we walked down this long hallway.

"Pregnant already, huh?" I heard Angela say under her breath.

I turned around and looked at Prince, and he ran his fingers across his lips, telling me to zip it. See, what Angela didn't know was she had already set the tone for this dinner. She was bound to get cursed out before the turkey even gets cut.

"Dinner will be ready in just a few, guys," Angela spoke.

We were all sitting in the living room having general conversation, and I was looking at the text messages that continued to come through my phone.

Duke: *Pilar, you really got me fucked up. I can't eat or sleep. I ain't know I needed you until I didn't have you. I'm sorry, please come home, so we can work this shit out.*

This nigga didn't have me for a month, so what the fuck is he talking about. This nigga was just talking right now.

Me: *Duke, now you talking fucking stupid. You a fuckin' lie. You left me in that house for a WHOLE month BY myself. YOU didn't talk to ME. I kept trying to apologize to YOU! You ignored me, then showed up with that bitch! You got me fucked up! Nigga, as far as I'm concerned, you can stay with that bitch, and we will figure out a way to co-parent. You do you and, nigga, I'mma do me. Talking about I ain't know what I had until I didn't…shut the fuck up, Duke. You better be glad I can't block your ass right now… Leave me the fuck alone.*

Duke: *You act like I ain't told you that I'll drop any and everybody for you. I told you that. You know you'll always have my heart. Always. No matter how bad shit get. You mine, man.*

"Pilar, so what do you do with yourself?" I looked up to Angela speaking to me.

"Nothing. I have a rich baby daddy, but I do go to the Salvation Army on Saturdays and feed the homeless," I replied.

She looked at me like I had two heads on my shoulders, and I smirked to myself.

"You have a degree, right?"

"Yes, I do! I'm not using it right now because I couldn't find a job. I did have a job, but I got fired because of some stupid mess, and I been cool ever since. I'll probably open a shelter or something when the twins are able to go to daycare."

"Interesting. You go to church?"

"No, but I believe. Maybe, I'll start. I could use some type of something right now."

"You can always use Jesus. Church is the…"

I blacked out after that. This was the reason why I don't go to church because I hated preachers who tried to tell me what I needed. No, bitch, don't tell me what I need. I looked at her mouth move, and all I heard was 'whomp, whomp, whomp.' I just slowly nodded my head, agreeing to whatever I thought she was saying. She could be saying that she was going to cut my head off, and I was just agreeing. The next thing I heard was someone say dinner was ready.

Surprisingly, and I do mean surprisingly, dinner went swell. After the tension was cut in the room, the dinner went well. I was glad they didn't ask me too many crazy questions. I didn't even have to curse them out. After dinner, we continued to talk and get to know each other. I could have easily got on their ass about that shit that Prince told me, but I heard Savannah's voice telling me not to hold people's past against them. I just wanted to hide here forever, but I knew I couldn't.

EDWINA

*D*ammmnnnnnn, I came here to fuck some shit up between that bitch and Duke not even knowing that Duke wasn't even fucking with her to begin with. I was in the corner with Fredrick, laughing at the way her friend was making a fool of herself in front of hundreds of people. That couldn't be me. This was the second time Duke had embarrassed her ass. If I was her, I would be done fucking with him. Pilar walked away with her tail between her legs, and my heart was filled with so much joy, although it shouldn't have been. She took him from me, and another bitch took him from her. It's funny how the world works. Whatever you put out into the universe, is what you are going to get back. I shouldn't be the one saying that, but whatever.

Fredrick loved the way I looked outside of my normal clothes. My make-over was everything. My hair stopped in the center of my back, but I got it cut into a short, Nicole Murphy style. I put on a fitted dress, but I still had a little pudge from having Brielle. I didn't tell Fredrick about my baby, and since I wouldn't see her again, it didn't even matter. We had been talking and hanging out for the last two weeks, and he was so fun to be around. I was a little down when he told me that he had a wife, but he said they were separated. He told me that he owned a club and a car lot. So, this nigga had a lot of money. I knew it wasn't a match to Duke's, but that would be fine. He told me that he would give me a job, and I was excited. I wasn't close to running out of money just yet, but when you are spending, and none is coming in, then you need to do something. I couldn't wait to give him some of this pussy. I knew he had a big dick because I sucked it after Duke's party. His shit was so big and wide, much bigger than Duke's, and I knew he was going to fuck me much better.

I had just got out of the shower when Fredrick called me and told me that he was downstairs. I told him to give me a couple of minutes, and I would be down in just a moment. I rushed to get dressed because it seemed like he hated when people are not on time. When I got on the elevator, I saw the girl from Duke's party and held the elevator for her.

"Hey, how are you?" I asked her, starting a conversation with her.

"I'm fine. How are you?" she replied, and she had an accent. "Where are you from?"

"I'm from Egypt," I replied.

"Seriously. My boyfriend is from there. Duke. He's the prince or whatever. I'm sure you know him," she smiled.

"Yeah, I know him." I shrugged. "Trust me, I know him really well."

"Hmph. We live in this building. Well, not really. He lives in this building, and I'm over all the time. I might as well move in with him. I like him a lot, and he takes care of me."

I rolled my eyes at that comment. Of course, he does. He loves women. Since we got on the elevator from the same floor, I was sure we lived on the same floor.

"Don't fall in love with him…too quick," I warned her.

"It's kind of late for that. The dick, the money…it's hard not to, but right now, he's been stressed about his baby mama. He won't even touch me right now. He has been staying at his other house while looking for her. She is fucking up shit. I'm jealous of her. She has no reason to be jealous of me. She got his kids, and he will always choose them over me."

She just kept talking, and I loved it. If I wasn't making shit work with Fredrick, I would be trying to scheme with her to get rid of Pilar, but I wasn't on that no more.

"Alright, girl. Well, I live in this building too. So, hopefully, we will be seeing each other around," I said as we stepped off the elevator.

Fredrick was waiting in front of the building. As soon as I opened the door to his car, she was running toward the car.

"I didn't get your name," she screamed, but I shut the door, pretending I didn't hear her.

WAP!

Fredrick's hand came across my face. My hand went to my stinging face. I thought about the first time that Dutch hit me, and I started hitting his ass back so fast. I was raining blows on him. I didn't leave Egypt to come here to endure the same thing that I endured from Dutch. He started swinging back until he latched on to my throat.

"Don't you ever put your fucking hands on me again," he growled in my face. "You making me waste money, having to sit out here and wait on your ass."

"Let me out," I screamed as loud as I could while clawing at his hands.

"I ain't letting you shit," he replied.

BAM!

He punched me in my face and knocked me out.

A few hours later...

I woke up, and my body was hurting so bad. I blinked my eyes to get used to the light, and I was surrounded by a whole bunch of naked women. I sat up in the bed, panicking, looking for my things.

"Where am I?" I asked no one in particular.

One girl replied, "Oh you're at Fred's house. We work for him. My name is Marshell. I run the house."

"No, I can't stay here. I have to get home," I panicked.

"Oh, baby. When you get with Fred, there is no going back unless you want to die. Come on, so I can show you around," she said.

"Why are we naked?" I whispered.

"Oh, we are always going to be naked around here. Yes, even when you are on your period, you are going to be naked. You just have to stick a tampon up your pussy and go on."

"How long have you been here?" I asked her.

"I have been here for seven years."

"I thought he had a wife and kids."

Marshell laughed extremely hard before replying, "Girl, he tells everybody that story. I believed it too."

We started walking through this big ass house. There were several bedroom doors with locks on them.

"This is where you will sleep. Listen, don't be scared. Fred really takes good care of us. We all have different jobs. You're reallllly pretty, so you're going to be working in the strip club."

"I have never stripped before. Where are my things? Where is my phone?"

"You don't get a phone here. You work and come home. You won't have time to talk to nobody else. I'm going to show you some moves, and you start tonight."

I instantly started crying because this was not what I wanted. I have been reduced from being with a prince to being with a fucking pimp. What the fuck?

"Don't cry. You will get used to it. I promise. Soon, you will be happy just like the other girls. Edwina, please don't try anything crazy because I would hate to see you get beat because you are sooo pretty. Okay?"

I nodded my head and walked in my new room.

"Whenever these doors closed, they lock. They can only be open with a key. So, they are to be left open until it is time for bed unless Fred or I come close them for whatever reason.

"What if there is a fire?"

"There will never be a fire," she said and turned to walk away.

I walked into the room, sat on the twin sized bed, and cried my eyes out. I didn't want this, and I thought Fred was a decent guy.

"Hey, why are you crying? You are going to like it here." I looked up and saw Fredrick standing at the door.

He walked in and closed the door. He sat next to me and started rubbing my back.

"Fredrick, this is not what I want. I don't want to be some pimp's girl. When I said, I wanted a job, I meant maybe like a server or something not a stripper. I didn't come over here for this."

He stared at me with a horrible scowl on his face. I didn't know what he was about to say, but I was hoping that he would let me go.

"Well, baby, it doesn't work that way. Once you step foot in that door, then you don't leave out unless it's death. Please, don't ever try to run either because I will find you," he said, grabbing my wrists. "You see this right here." He pointed at the scar that was now on my wrists. "That means, I own you. This tracker lets me know where you always are, darling. Now, lay back. Let me give you a proper welcome."

I just stared at his back as he got up to close the door. I saw that the keys were on his waist like he was a damn janitor. I was rubbing my wrist where the tracker was. I was not anyone's property, but I was going to play this damn part like an actress until I could get out of here. I laid back on the bed and smiled at him. I spread my pussy lips open for him, and he started grinning like a damn Cheshire cat.

"See, that's the damn spirit right there. You are going to fit in perfectly here, girl. You know that," he said as he got on his knees in front of me.

He got on his knees and started licking my pussy like this was his first time eating a pussy. It was so annoying, but I moaned, pretending to be into that shit. He stopped eating me after five minutes. Who does that shit? He pulled his shorts down and started stroking his big dick. He straddled me and pushed inside of me roughly. This was not what I pictured our first time being like. I always thought that it would be more special than this. I closed my eyes as he continued to jab inside of me and pictured that it was the first man that I fell in love with... Duke.

DUKE

*W*hen Pilar went missing, that fucked me up in so many ways. She wasn't answering her phone for anybody, not even her friends. I was sick as fuck. I just couldn't get that chick out my system. No matter how much Mandee sucked my dick or clamped her pussy around my dick. I just couldn't get that girl off my mind. I tried so many times. I haven't seen her since my party, but I know she's back because she texted me the time of the appointment.

"Mandee, chill. I gotta go," I said, trying to move her out the way. "I can't be late."

"The appointment is not for another twenty minutes, you won't be late. Just put it in me for about five minutes."

Truth is, I didn't want to be late, but I also wanted a chance to talk to her before we went to the back. I knew that we wouldn't be able to talk once we get in the doctor's office because his ass talked too damn much.

"Nah, you can get it all when I get back, aight?"

I kissed her forehead, and she had a sad look on her face. I already knew what that was about. She knows that the twins are almost here, and my main focus is going to be Pilar and the twins. I was going to be over there like ninety-five percent of the time. She kept trying to solidify her place in my life by fucking and sucking me. She was a real cool chick, but if she could handle my life after these kids were born, then she may be a keeper, BUT that was only if I could fully get over Pilar. I must know for a fucking fact that I had absolutely no chance of getting back with her.

"Oh, I forgot to tell you that I met a girl here the other day that says she know you very well. She was a pretty light skinned girl from Egypt as well. She had very short hair and a little thick."

My eyebrows immediately went up because that couldn't be who I thought it was, but I had to be sure.

"Um, did you get her name?"

"No, she was getting in a car when I tried to get it. She lives in this building. I haven't seen her since that day, though. Weird. It might have something to do with that guy because it looked like they got into a fight when she shut the door of the car, but don't worry about it. Next time I see her, I'll get her name."

"Aight," I said and walked out the door.

I went into the garage and hopped in my car. Since I only had a few minutes to talk, I decided to call Bakari back because he had called me several times back to back about two weeks ago, but I didn't answer. This nigga answered on the first ring.

"Duke, I'm glad you called me back. I have something to tell you."

"Go 'head."

"Edwina is in Jacksonville. She called me, crying and shit. I just wanted to let you know because I don't know if she on some revenge shit. Aight?"

"Cool." I was getting ready to press the end button on my steering wheel.

"Duke, I love you, bro! For real. I know you getting tired of me apologizing, but what can I do for you to..."

I pressed the end button. I wasn't trying to hear that shit. Speaking of, Dutch's ass was still in the dungeon, losing weight by the damn week. I still hadn't thought about what I wanted to do to him yet. I just made sure my granddad keeps him alive. Bakari's fate was in the hands of Pilar, but she ain't told me what she wanted me to do with him just yet.

As I was pulling in the damn doctor's office, Pilar's ass was getting out of a brand-new Mercedes. She had gotten much bigger, and she had her hair into a curly ball on top of her head. She looked like she was struggling. She had on a long maxi dress with flip flops. I parked my car and got out. When I approached her, I could tell that her skin was glowing. She looked happy.

"Pilar, baby, how are you doing? You look good to be eight months pregnant with twins. Your feet are not cold with those flip flops on?"

I was asking any and everything just to hear her say anything. I hadn't heard her voice in I don't know how long.

"My feet are not cold. These kids keep me hot enough to not even turn the heat on in my house." She smiled.

We went and got checked in. I helped her into her seat, and then I sat down.

"Pilar, we really need to..."

"Oh, shit!"

"What?" I panicked. "Is everything okay?"

She nodded her head, took my hand, and placed it on her stomach. The twins were moving around something serious in there. I was rubbing her stomach on one side while she was tapping on the other side.

"Aye, girl, don't be whoopin' on my kids, man. They ain't doing nothing but what they supposed to do," I said to her, and she laughed.

"Chile, you ain't gon' be there every day, so when they get older, I'mma be tearing they ass up."

Damn, that was a low-blow. I guess that was her way of telling me that we ain't gon' get back together. Before I could reply, they called her to the back. We went to the back, and they got her vital signs, and I helped her up onto the table. That smiling ass nigga walked in the room.

"Ms. Harrison, you took a big break from me, and that was not safe. You were to far long to be on that airplane. You really hurt Savannah's feelings. She didn't know if it was something she said or what. Good afternoon, Mr. Ramses."

I spoke to him. I was hoping that they would keep talking because she still ain't told anyone where she went.

"I know. I just needed a moment alone. I felt suffocated being here at that moment, and I just needed a break."

"Alright, lay back. We are finally going to figure out what you are having. Also, it's time for you to start seeing me once a week. Pilar, you might not make it to January twentieth."

"Doc, don't say that. I'm still trying to get their nurseries set up," she replied.

I didn't want to say anything because we were still in the doctor's office, but I didn't know where she thought she was staying, but she wasn't about to stay by herself. Not with my kids.

"Alright! Sorry, I don't want to jinx anything. What do you want to have?" he asked.

"My grandma said that it's going to be a boy and a girl."

"Grandma?" I asked.

"It's a long story. I'll tell you later," she said.

He turned the ultrasound machine on, and my kids were in her stomach damn near hugging. I looked at Pilar, and she was crying.

"Dr. Keys, I want multiple pictures of that ultrasound, please."

"Okay, it looks like your grandmother was right. You are having a boy and a girl."

I teared up at the thought of having a son. Man, this was going to be crazy. I could already see myself playing basketball with him. This was going to be perfect. Then, I'm having a daughter too. The Lord knew He was funny. Man, I was about to go buy some more guns, especially if she looks like her sexy ass mama. Damn! I wiped my eyes with the back of my hand.

"Pilar, have you been walking? It will make your birth easier. Have you decided on what type of birth you want to do? Will you be getting an epidural?"

The doctor shot off question after question. Pilar looked confused, and I forgot that I had to answer questions for my baby because she gets frustrated fast.

"Doctor, she will not be getting any medications to assist her with her birth. She will be having a water birth, and we will be keeping the placenta for six hours after the birth. After that, you can do whatever it is that you all do with that."

"Pilar," the doctor looked at her.

"Baby daddy has spoken."

"Well, let me get you cleaned up, and I will see you next week," Dr. Keys said.

∞

"So, Pilar, what are we going to do about living arrangements? I want to wake up with my kids and go to sleep with my kids. We ain't really got much time to decide," I said to her as we walked around buybuy BABY.

We decided that we needed to talk, so we decided to shop for the twins and talk at the same time. Her ass hadn't said much since we came in here. She stopped by a stroller set.

"I like this, do you?" she asked.

"Yeah, I like whatever you like, but stop playing. What are we going to do?"

"Well, Duke, you are the one who thought that we should have different living arrangements. You are the one that moved out, got a girlfriend, and whatever. I didn't want to live there without you and definitely since we not together. So, the babies are going to stay with me at my place, and I guess you can come over early and leave late. I don't know. I don't want your girlfriend to get the wrong idea."

"Man, she ain't my girlfriend. We just cool."

"Cool enough to be living together, right? I don't want to talk about that. You figure out what you want to do. I'm open to whatever unless I start dating seriously or something. Then, you won't be able to stay over."

Tensing up at the thought of her dating someone else, I had to take a few deep breaths and change the damn subject before I went off on her ass thinking she was about to date when she just had my kids.

"So, where did you go?"

"I went to my dad's. Yeah, I know right. It sounds really weird coming out of my mouth, but we really got to know each other and my grandparents too. I mean, Prince and I talk mostly every day, and his mom calls every other day. I guess we are making up for lost time," she said.

"Speaking of, I have something that belongs to you, but it's back home. When I go back over there, I will bring it to you. I don't know when I'll be going back over there since you are getting ready to have the babies. I don't want to get over there and your ass goes into labor."

"Okay, that's fine. I know you are wondering, but my dad bought me a three-bedroom condo on the beach, and he bought me that car."

"Nah, I wasn't really wondering that," I lied like a mothafucka. "You and the kids are going to have a driver anyway, so I wasn't really worried."

"Duke, I'm not going to be helpless. Your girlfriend is going to be mad at you," she teased.

Pulling her chin up to look at me, I stared deep into her catlike eyes.

"Baby, you will always be THE number one lady in my life. Well, you 'bout to be number two when my daughter born. Ain't no woman gon' come between that shit, and if said woman doesn't understand that, then later for her."

Her eyes welled up with tears, but she was giving me THE look. The look that told me that she needed me inside of her. She needed to stop looking at me like that before I took her right here in this damn store. My phone ringing made us break that trance. I looked at it, and it was Mandee. I didn't answer it. I was sure she was looking for me because I told her that I would be back after the appointment. We had been in that damn store for two hours, and we had two carts full of shit.

"Maybe we should go," she whispered.

"Did you not just hear what the fuck I said to you? You first in my life."

She smiled a little as we made our way to the register. We had so much shit that we literally had three people ringing up our shit at one time. We spent thousands in that damn store, and she told me that she wasn't done. She said that her grandparents had ordered car seats and cribs. We packed all the shit in both cars and headed to her condo. On the way to the condo, we passed by her and Swan's old house. After we found the camera that the nigga had in the house, I instantly made

Pilar change her number, and Baron made Swan move out to Ramses Avenue. She probably wanted to be out there anyway.

I thought I was going to have to make several trips, but her condo building had a big ass cart that we could set the bags on and take the elevator up to her floor. We unloaded the cart in her condo, and I took it back to the elevator and sent it back down. When I walked back inside, Pilar had taken off her dress, and she had on a matching Calvin Klein bra and boy short set. That seemed to be her favorite bra set.

"Sorry, I'm just always hot now. Thank you for everything, Duke," she said as she flipped through the channels on the TV.

"You ain't got to thank me. That's what I'm supposed to do."

She went sat on the couch after she found something to watch on the TV. I sat next to her. I didn't want to go home. This was the longest that we have been in each other presence in a long time, and I wanted to savor the moment. She didn't say anything, but she scrunched her face up. I was getting ready to ask her what was wrong until I saw my kids in her stomach having a field day. I started rubbing her stomach.

"Are they always like this?" I asked.

"Not normally, but today they have been overly active. They need to go to sleep because they are coming out on a schedule. Wake in the day and sleep at night. I ain't playing no games."

There was that stare again. Moving slowly toward her face, I placed my lips on hers. She placed her hand on the back of my head, holding me in place. As our tongues danced in each other's mouth. I could feel myself falling deeper and deeper in love with her. I would never be able to stop loving her. I pulled at the waistband of her panties and stuck my hand between her legs, and she was wet as hell. Damn! I pulled away from her and helped her out of her panties and bra.

"You're so beautiful, Pilar. Damn!" I whispered to her, and I kissed all over her neck. I put my head in between her big juicy ass titties. They had grown like two cup sizes. I just wanted to juggle them. I kissed all the way down to her love box. I started eating her like it was going out of style. Her clit was so fucking swollen. One flick of my tongue across her clit, and she was cumming. She was moaning like crazy, and it was making my dick harder and harder. I came up and stared at her.

"Pilar, are you sure you want to do this?"

I had to ask because the last time I did this, her ass started crying, and I woke up to her ass riding my damn dick. So, I didn't know.

"Yes, I need it!"

She got up and put her knees on the couch, holding on to the back of the couch. I placed myself behind her and pushed slowly into her tight, wet walls. Just my luck, she had a mirror leaning against the wall, and I had a good view of us. She knew how much I loved mirrors.

"Damn, baby, look at me," I ordered as I bit into her shoulder.

She looked up into the mirror, and we locked eyes. Thrusting in and out of her slowly, I placed wet kisses all over her neck and back. Pilar was so wet that she was leaking down my leg.

"I missed this… I need this. I love you so much! You know that?" I whispered as I looked her dead in her eyes.

"I love you too, daddyyy. Damn, I'm cummiinnggg!"

"I know, baby! I know, baby! I feel you! Fuck! Daddy cumming too!"

I thrust into her one more time, and I shot my nut inside of her. We stayed in that position for a minute, staring at each other in the mirror.

"Can I stay here tonight?" I asked.

"You know you can't stay here. Duke, we gotta do shit the right way. You have a woman, and what we just did was wrong."

"You right, mama. I don't regret it at all, though. I'll see you next week, okay?"

I placed sweet kisses all over her face, and then our lips connected again.

"Just for tonight, Duke. Just...for...tonight," she whispered against my lips.

I happily obliged. I walked her to her room, and I made sweet love to her on and off for the rest of the night.

PILAR

*L*ast night with Duke was nothing short of amazing, but I was wrong. I knew I was, but it was what I needed. After one more round of sex this morning, I sent him home to deal with his chick. I got up and took a long hot shower. I put on a yellow maxi dress along with my flip flops. Maxi dresses and flip flops had become a staple because who knew being pregnant would just make you hot all the damn time. Even in the damn winter time, my body temperature was above normal. I had my last appointment with Savannah before the new year since this week was Christmas.

I made sure I looked good because I had a date with Ryder right after the appointment. I grabbed my purse and headed out the door. With Christmas being close, traffic was jam packed, and it was annoying. After my date, I was going out with Swan and Lee because we needed to catch up. I invited them over to the condo the first night I came back IF they promised they wouldn't tell their niggas, and they did. We argued for the first hour, and after that, we were friends again.

After being in stuck in traffic, I finally made it to Savannah's office. I checked in, and Savannah was already at the front. When I got in her office, I continued to walk around instead of sitting down. She had a big enough office so I wouldn't have to walk in small circles.

"So, any reason why you are doing that?" Savannah asked.

"Well, Dr. Keys said that I need to start walking, and I might as well start right now," I replied.

"Girl, come sit down. You can walk later. Tell me what's been going on."

"Well, you are going to be mad at me, but I had sex with Duke all last night and one time this morning. We both understood that what we did was wrong, and it's not going to happen again. I'm truly in a great space right now, seriously. When I was away, I got to know my dad's side of the family, and I forgave him. We talk every day. We are getting there. So, your sessions have been working. I do listen. I am going on a date with Ryder when I leave here and having a girls' date later after that."

"I'm not used to you admitting you were wrong, so I don't even have a spill here. I'm so excited that you took the first step to meeting the other side of your family.

"However, there is one hitch, though. Duke said that he wants to wake up to his kids and go to sleep to his kids, and I told him that is something that he gotta work out with his girlfriend. I told him that I don't have a problem, but if I start dating, he couldn't stay the night and all of that shit. So, what I should do?"

"Well, that is a dilemma. Do you think that is safe for you two as far as you both dating other people? Do you think that you would be able to control yourself around him? I know you are still in love with him."

"I am, Savannah. I am still in love with him, but I'm moving past it. I don't think I will be able to see them together right now, but for now, I'm doing good. I'm not mad at her nor will I ever be. You don't have to worry about me beating her ass unless she steps to me."

"Just continue to work on yourself, and you will be fine. Although, I don't approve of you dating Ryder now, but you are going to do what you want to do. I hope you know what you are doing."

"I knooooowww, Duke, and that's the thing. When I legit start dating someone, he's going to become unhinged, and it's not fair, especially since they are living together now. I'mma see how it goes, and I will text you, okay!?"

"Be safe, Pilar. I will see you next year."

"Are you going to come to the hospital when the twins are born? I'm having a boy and a girl. I don't have names yet."

"Are you giving me permission? I can't speak to you in public unless you say something to me first."

"Y'all got a lot of dumb rules, but yeah, you can come."

She laughed and gave me a hug. I left the office feeling refreshed.

Ryder and I agreed to meet at the restaurant that was around the corner from Savannah's office. He was there before me, and he waved me over. I waddled over to him, and he gave me the biggest embrace. Jesus Christ, this man was looking so sexy in this damn tailored suit. I had been texting Ryder when I was in Mississippi. He texted me on Thanksgiving, and we haven't stopped talking since.

"You look beautiful, you know that?" Ryder asked.

This is my first time seeing him since that last time I saw him in his office. I mean, I had cut him off since I thought that Duke and I were going to make things work, but things didn't work out.

"Oh, you're being modest. I am getting ready to pop like a damn balloon," I said, as he pulled my chair out for me.

"I am not being modest, baby. Damn! That curly hair does something to me," he said and had me blushing like a school girl.

I already knew what I wanted because I'd been here a thousand times, and so did Ryder.

"So, how was work? I know you are always busy and shit."

"Busy is what keeps me in business, baby girl. Work was work. A lot of paperwork and stuff. I'm happy for this Christmas and New Year's break. Although, this is when people go to jail THE most, and I will probably won't get a full break." He chuckled.

"That's messed up."

My phone alerted me that I had a text message, and I checked it.

Babydaddy: Where the fuck are you?

Me: On a date. What you need?

Babydaddy: A DATE? Pilar, are you fucking serious? You about to have my fucking kids in less than probably two weeks, and you on a date. Take yo' mothafuckin' ass home, and get in the fucking bed, or walk around or some shit.

Me: I'm about to have your kids in less than probably two weeks, and you have a whole girlfriend. Mama gotta have a life, too, lol. I'll let you know when I get home.

Babydaddy: Hehe hell. I'mma handcuff your ugly ass to the fucking bed. Try me, you big head mothafucka you. You can't date until my kids are 'least one.

Me: *Nah. I'm dating now. Bye.*

I put my phone in my purse and ignored the continuous vibrations against my leg. Ryder and I talked for the next two hours. Ryder was making me laugh, and it was exactly what I needed to get my mind off Duke. He never once asked about Duke, which meant that he probably wasn't threatened by his ass.

"Well, I'm going to get home, Ryder. I wish I knew when we would go on another date because these kids are going to be coming soon, and I..."

He stopped me from talking and placed a kiss on my lips. His lips were so soft, and he pushed his tongue inside of my mouth. Ryder assaulted me with his lips, and he had every hair on my body standing up. He pulled back, and we stared at each other.

"Wow! Wow!"

"I'm willing to wait for you, baby girl," he whispered.

He dropped money on the table and walked me to the car. He said that was going to make sure that I got home safe. While he was following me, we were talking on the phone. He even followed me into the garage and waited until I parked my car. He said that he was going to stay on the phone until I got upstairs. As I was walking toward the elevator, Ryder watched me. Duke's ugly ass was pacing in front of the elevator.

"You know him?" Ryder asked into the phone.

"Yeah, it's the twins' dad," I groaned.

As I got closer to the elevator, Duke noticed me and went slap off.

"Get the fuck off the phone. Tell your boy toy you good," Duke snapped.

"You okay?" Ryder asked. He hadn't pulled out of the garage yet.

"Yes, it's fine. Seriously, he's harmless to me. I'll talk to you later."

After I reassured him that I was okay, I hung up the phone, and he drove away. I pressed the code for the elevator and got on with Duke on my heels.

"Your nigga making sure you get home safe?" he spat.

"That would be the gentleman thing to do, Duke," I replied.

We rode the elevator up in silence, but I could feel the steam coming off his body. I wanted to laugh so bad because this nigga was jealous. On the inside, I was doing backflips.

"I think it's time that I introduce you to Mandee," he said as I sat my purse on the bar.

I knew he was trying to get under my skin and shit, but at this point, it was whatever. We could both play the damn game.

Turning to look at him straight in his eyes, I said, "Duke, that is fine. If she is going to be the woman in your life, that means she is going to be in my children's life. So, it's only right that I meet her." I smiled at him.

That left eye started twitching, and I turned around to get a bottle of water out the fridge.

"You serious as fuck right now?"

"Duke, I'm about as serious as serious gets right now."

When I turned around Duke was on his knees. He started rolling my dress up, and before I could even stop him, he was sucking on my pussy through my panties. He pulled them to the side and pushed two fingers inside of me. I grabbed on to his shoulders, trying to keep my balance.

"You think that nigga gon' make you cum like you doing now? Look at you, creaming up my fingers," Duke growled.

"Ahh, shit!"

"Look at me! Who can make you cum like me? WHO?"

My legs were getting weak, and my pussy continued to run like a faucet. I couldn't answer his question. I had to close my eyes from all the pleasure that I was feeling.

"WHO gon' make this pussy cum, Pilar, huh? Look at ME! WHO?" he growled.

I stared into his eyes as I came hard.

"You, baby! Fuck!"

He got up, turned me around, and placed my hands on the counter. He entered me slowly and started giving me looonnnggg deep strokes, making my damn eyes cross.

"P, whenever you ready to stop playing games, I'm here, baby. Me." *Long stroke.* "You." *Short stroke.* "The twins." *Two long strokes.* "A family. Our family."

"Dadddyyy, I'm in looovveee with you! Fuckk!"

"I'm morrrree in love with you. Can I fuck you just a little harder?

Just a little harder, please," he begged.

"Just a little. Just a little! Fuck!"

Duke thrusted and grinded inside of me until we both came at the same time. We were both breathing hard. I turned to look at him, and he was giving me that look. That look that told me that he wanted to stay, and of course, my dumb ass gave in.

DUKE

$\mathcal{A}$ll those promises I made Pilar about us being together was the fucking truth. I'm in love with her, and that shit ain't gon' ever change. That shit pissed me off when she said that she was on a date, though. When I woke up this morning, I put the cribs that her grandparents sent together. While I was putting them together, Pilar came and leaned in the doorway. She had on a silk robe, and she was naked underneath.

"Thank you for putting those together. I was going to call one of your brothers, but thank you," she said.

"Girl, don't call those niggas before you call me. Pilar, is it weird that I think you are so fucking sexy carrying my kids? Damn! I mean, you were already sexy, but I mean... damn. This pregnancy is making you glow. When you have the twins, the minute you can have sex again, I'm getting you pregnant again."

"Shut up. You got a girlfriend. You need to get home. I'm sure she is wondering where you are. What happened when you went home?"

"Not shit you need to worry about."

Truth was, Mandee didn't even snap at me, which was weird and not what I was expecting. She was there cooking me breakfast and shit. I was scared to even eat that shit in fear that she probably tried to poison a nigga or something, but she didn't.

"Alright! Well, I'm about to go up to the gym and walk a mile around the track. Lock up when you leave."

Before I could answer, she left the doorway. Moments later she walked back by with her sports bra on and some short Nike shorts. My baby was literally all belly. I heard the door close. When I finished with the cribs, I did as she said and locked up when I left. I went up to the gym to get me a kiss before I left, and when I made it up there, she was walking around the track with some big cock diesel mothafucka.

"Pilar," I yelled her name.

She and the guy made their way over to me. I was pissed off. She was glistening with sweat.

"Hey, baby daddy! Everything okay? Did you lock up?" she asked.

"Yeah, who the fuck is this?" I asked through gritted teeth.

"Duke, this is Ryder, and Ryder this is Duke, the twins' father."

Ryder extended his hand, but I just looked at it like it was covered in shit.

"Ryder, can you excuse us for a second, please?" Pilar said and pulled me out the door. "What is your problem, Duke? You are going to introduce me to Mandee."

"How the fuck you was just riding my damn tongue last night and now you up here with this big eighteen wheeler looking ass nigga. You foul!" I shouted.

"You better lower your voice, Duke. The same way I was gargling your fucking nuts in my mouth last night, and you got a girlfriend AT HOME! He and I are not fucking. He and I are not living together. We are dating. That's it. Not even in comparison to what you are doing with Mandee. You better chill."

"You got it, Pilar," I said and walked away from her.

When I got in my car, I called my brothers and told them that we were going out tonight. I needed to relieve some damn pressure before I ended up killing my damn baby mama. I made it home, and Mandee was sitting in a pile of my bleached clothes.

"Mandee, what the fuck are you doing? Why you bleach my shit."

"WHY THE FUCK ARE YOU TREATING ME LIKE THIS? YOU APPROACHED ME KNOWING THAT YOU ARE STILL FUCKING WITH YOUR BABY MAMA. I SMELL HER FUCKING PUSSY ALL OVER YOU. WHY AM I HERE?" Mandee yelled.

"I wasn't fucking with her at the time. Why the fuck did you bleach my shit? Mandee, get your shit and get the fuck out."

"How could you do this to me? I put my life on hold on for you. I could have been out dating men who want to marry me and give me kids."

"Wait, let's dial it back a little. Mandee, I'm having twins soon, and I won't even have time for a relationship let alone a marriage and more kids."

"Shut the fuck up! You make time for what you want to make time for. You only using me as a placeholder until that bitch takes you back."

WAP!

Before I knew it, I had back slapped her off her knees.

"Don't you ever fucking disrespect the mother of my kids, and to think, I was going to take your ass to meet her. You got me fucked up now. I'm leaving, and when I come back, I want your ass the fuck up out of here."

I turned to leave, and this girl started hitting me in my back. She jumped on my back and tried to choke me from the back. I pulled her around my neck, and she was facing me, but she still had her legs wrapped around me. I grabbed her arms and placed them above her head.

"Look, I'm sorry for hurting you. That is my fault, but if you hit me again, I'm gon' beat your ass. I should beat your ass after bleaching my shit, but I ain't gon' do it," I spat, and pushed her ass on the couch.

I left out the house and headed to Ramses Avenue. I walked into Baron's house, and he had Swan bent over the couch fucking the shit out of her.

"Damn, bro! You need to knock, nigga," Baron snapped.

I turned around and looked at the wall until they got dressed. He sent Swan upstairs and told me that I could turn around. I sat in the chair, and he stared at me.

"What, nigga?" I snapped.

"Man, you came over here, fucked up my session, and sitting here not saying shit. What the fuck you want? We still got a minute before we go out. The fuck you want?"

"Y'all can fuck any time, nigga. Man, I'm in love with Pilar."

His eyes moved from side to side and then squinted. He genuinely looked confused.

"Ummm, okay. Did you just have an epiphany or something? Why are you telling me something that I already know? Wait a minute, did you just come wayyyy over here to tell me that. You fucking with me, ain't you?"

"Nah, I ain't fucking with you. I'm just in love with her, and I want to make it right with her."

"Okay, you did mess up pretty bad. You got a lot to making up to do. You were very petty, Duke. Let me tell you something. You didn't even try to help her get through her..."

"What the fuck? She threw what I told her back in my face and in front of her pussy ass doctor," I cut him off.

"That was childish. You ain't even talk to her after that. You left, got another girlfriend, and then she found out in front of hundreds of people, JUST like back home when she found out about Edwina. Everything that is going wrong with your relationship with the mother of my niece and nephew is YOUR fault. YOUR...fault. YOUR..."

"I get it, mothafucka."

"No, I don't think you do. Let me run down what you did to her. First things first, you didn't let her know that you had a fiancée and a baby on the way. Then you tried to be slick and bring her to Egypt like she wouldn't find out. Second, your ass did NOT believe her when she said she was raped. You physically abused her, left her ALONE for a whole month with no conversation, got another girlfriend, damn near moved her in. I literally lost count of what you did to her. Then your ass wanted to cry when she went to visit her dad for a few days. You better be lucky that she even still wants to deal with your ass. Honestly, bro! You don't deserve her."

"Man, don't say that shit. She's already dating some big ass nigga. He took her out on a date yesterday. I fucked her last night, and she was walking with him this morning. I could see by the way that he was looking at her that he's falling for her. I can't have that, man."

"Bruh, let her move on. If you love her, then you need to let her move on. As cliché as this sounds, if y'all are meant to be, then you guys will get back together. Y'all need a break from each other, and you need some counseling. You need to learn how to help her cope with what happened to her. You, yourself, need some counseling after all that shit that was said in that basement. You're hurt, and she's hurt. Two hurt people can only do what? Hurt each other. Now, let me go jump back in my girl's pussy because I just gave you too long of a serious talk, and I'm starting to feel different." He laughed. "I'll be ready by ten-thirty. Get out my house, nigga."

Damn, everything Baron said was right. I'm so used to being the big brother and having to bottle shit up that it spilled over into my relationship. I was wrong for doing Pilar the way that I did her, and I was wrong for stringing Mandee along. She didn't do anything but try and be a good woman to me. I prayed that I didn't mess her up for the next guy because she was a good woman. I guess like Baron said, it wouldn't hurt to get counseling. Savannah seemed like a good woman, and she really relaxed Pilar. Maybe, it wouldn't hurt to give her call. She could help me make some sense of this shit.

EDWINA

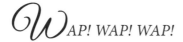AP! WAP! WAP!

Fredrick was beating my ass for trying to run away. This was my second time running away, and he caught me. My body still ached from the previous bruises on my body.

"See, you make me do this shit to you. How can you make money when your ass always in the house bruised the fuck up? You better bring home two thousand dollars tonight, or I'mma make you wish you was dead. Now, get fucking ready, and you better be able to conceal those bruises, hoe," Fredrick spat before walking out of the room.

Marshell came in right after him.

"Edwina, honey! What did I tell you about trying to run? You can't get away from him. You just need to accept this, and your life will be so much easier," she whispered.

I silently cried and prayed to myself that if I ever got out of this situation, I would turn my life around a hundred percent.

"Stop crying. I have to make sure that your make up is on point because if another customer complains about your bruising, he will probably kill you, regardless of you being his top money maker."

"I don't want to be here," I whispered.

"Well, you are going to learn. After a year or so, it will be just like clockwork."

This bitch must've been crazy. I would be gone before a year was up either by fleeing or death. I nodded my head with a smile. I was going to play my role.

"It's the holidays, and a lot of people are in town, so you are going to make that two thousand plus more tonight. We might get to go shopping. Well, you won't because you are going to run."

After she got me ready, she left out of the room. I prayed one more time before I heard the bell that alerted us to come down stairs. I grabbed my long jacket and fell in line with the rest of the girls. We were put in the back of the van and taken to the club. Once we got in that nasty funky ass locker room or wherever you called it, I changed into a thong bikini.

I took two shots of alcohol before I walked on the floor. The club was crowded. The girls were everywhere, and I was trying to figure out where I wanted to start.

"I wouldn't be standing here if I knew I had to make two thousand dollars or die," Fredrick growled.

I walked out on the floor, and one guy pulled me on his lap. He was ugly, and he stank. I wanted to gag. Before the song was over, I scanned the room looking for my next man. When I spotted Duke and his brothers, I almost cried tears of joy. The song changed, and the nigga put the money in my thong. I moved along and tried to make it to Duke, but someone grabbed me. I wanted to snatch away, but I didn't want that nigga to tell Fredrick.

Three songs later, I finally made it close to Duke. I was sure he probably couldn't tell it was me because of my short haircut. As soon as the song changed, I walked quickly and jumped in Duke's lap. I turned my head so he couldn't see my face. I leaned over to his ear and started speaking in our language because I didn't know if Fredrick put a listening device on me as well.

"Duke, please give me two minutes to talk. I know you hate me, but you have to save me. Grab my right wrist, and there is a tracker inside of it. I moved here, got mixed up with a pimp, and he kidnapped me and moved me in his house. I'm stuck. Please, help me. I will never bother you again."

He pushed me back and got a good look in my face. I kept grinding my hips.

"Edwina, what the fuck? Get off me," Duke growled.

"Noooo, please. I need your help."

"Stop fucking dancing on me, you stupid ass bitch. I oughta kill you up in here," he tried to move me.

"Duke, just dig the tracker out of my wrist, and I will make a run for it. Please. I can't do it on my own. I bitch up every time. Please. I'm going to hold my wrist down. Dig it out, and I'll leave."

I could tell that he was thinking about it. He grabbed my wrist and observed it. He threw it back down to my side, and by now his brothers had stopped paying attention to their women and looked at me.

"Edwina," Bomani called my name, but I ignored him.

"This is what the fuck you get, dumb bitch. You played me, and somebody played you. Get the fuck off me, and I'm only going to say it one more time."

I grabbed the knife off his table and started jabbing it into my wrist. Blood was getting on me and on him. His brothers tried to pull me off of him, but I hooked my arm around his neck. We were starting to attract attention, and I could feel myself getting weak.

"Man, FUCK! Come on y'all," Duke ordered.

He picked me up, wrapped his coat around me, and proceeded to the door before he was stopped.

"Where you going with her, my man? This is the property of Fredrick," I heard his voice, and he tried to snatch me away.

"She is also my wife, and I have been looking for her. If you don't get your hands off her, I'mma knock your ass out," Duke spat.

"I'mma find you, bitch!" Fredrick snapped. "You'll be dead before the sun rises," he yelled at Duke's back.

Duke put me in the back of the truck, and we sped toward the hospital. He carried me into the emergency room, and they immediately took me out of his arms. They put me behind the curtain, and I immediately told them everything that had happened and for them to call the police.

Duke watched as they dug the little tracking device out of my arm. I looked at him to see if I could gauge the way that he was feeling, but he didn't say anything. The police came in and took my statement. I told them that I didn't feel safe with him out of jail, and before I could even ask Duke for help, he walked out of the room. I guess that was as far as his help was going to go for me. At least, I had something to be thankful for.

PILAR

Christmas Day…

$\mathcal{T}$oday is awful. It wasn't awful because I didn't get any gifts or because I was surrounded by family. It was awful because these kids were giving me the blues with a capital B. The pain was something serious in my lower back to the point where I couldn't even get out the damn bed. I told Duke about the pain, and he made me come to his house and get in the bed. So, I have been in the bed while everyone was downstairs drinking alcohol, playing games, and opening gifts. I was mad as fuck, to be honest.

Knock! Knock!

"Hey, baby mama. How are you⌧"

"Ohhh."

"Pilar, you are scaring me. You sure you not going into labor. You ain't finna mess up my sheets with all that blood."

I laughed, and the pain hit me again.

"Can you call, Dr. Keys, please?" I asked.

Duke had the phone up to his ear, and then put him on

speakerphone.

"Hello, Pilar, this is Dr. Keys. How are you feeling?"

"Ohhh," I moaned. "My lower back hurts. I can't move. I've been in the bed all day."

"Come into the hospital for me, okay? You may be going into labor."

Duke hung up the phone before I could reply. He helped me out the bed. He grabbed the bag, and we walked out in the living room.

"Pilar's in labor, y'all!" Duke yelled in excitement.

Everybody jumped up and started moving around. Everybody started asking me a thousand questions. Duke helped me in the car, and he sped to the hospital. I wobbled in the hospital, and the nurse brought me a wheelchair. Dr. Keys was waiting for me. Duke helped me up on the bed, and I laid back. Instead of Duke sitting down, he was standing over Dr. Keys, which made him turn around and look at him.

"Dr. Keys, can you tell me what to feel for? I don't want you sticking your fingers in her. You might get some ideas, and I don't wanna knock you out," Duke said.

"Mr. Ramses, you are not the only father who has said that. I get it all the time," Dr. Keys said as he pushed a finger inside of me.

"Duke, shut up and sit down," I said.

"Pilar, you are in labor, but you are only dilated two centimeters. When you get ten centimeters, you will be able to push. These babies can come tonight or next week. It depends. It's really a definite when your water breaks. It's important to monitor your contractions as well."

"Damn, Dr. Keys. Tonight and next week is a hell of a gap."

He laughed before he walked out of the room. I groaned because I needed to get these babies out of me. He was going to send me home.

Walking back out into the lobby, my people were waiting for us.

"Damn, sis, no offense, but you still look pregnant," Bomani said and started cackling.

"Shut up, nigga. She's in labor, though, but not much. The doctor said tonight or next week."

In the car, Duke started telling me how he ran into Edwina in the strip club, and that she was running from a pimp. He told me that he took her to a hospital and left before she could ask for any more help.

"Damn, out of all the niggas in Jacksonville, she runs into a pimp. Damn. What was his name? Has he been arrested?"

"Nah, he hasn't been arrested yet. He's on the run, and his name was Fredrick."

"OH MY GOD! Was he light skin and like medium height? If so, that is who I bought my damn car from. He told me that he had a strip club. It is such a small world. I'm glad you helped her, Duke. I don't like that girl, but nobody deserves to be held against their will."

"Damn! Small world. Man, it's a good thing your ass didn't go on a date with him or something. Your ass could have been bruised up and shit, dancing for chump change."

"Yeah, right!" I said.

He didn't need to know about that little ten minute date we had before I jumped up and beat the fuck out of Demarkus and his wife.

Speaking of him, I wondered if his wife delivered her baby. That's probably why he hasn't found my number and harassed me lately, and I was so very thankful.

"So, Pilar, what's ol' dude like? The big dude," Duke asked.

He seemed so genuine to me, so I decided to answer.

"*Ryder* is nice. He's very nice and really caters to my feelings, even though I have been very hormonal lately. He's a lawyer and works downtown."

"Pilar, I'm happy that you are happy. Truly." He picked my hand up and kissed the back of it.

"Thank you, Duke. I really appreciate it. It means so much to me."

After we pulled up to the house, Duke helped me in the house and put me back in bed. He continued to check on me periodically throughout the night, and I was so thankful. Duke was truly going to be a great dad.

DUKE

New Year's Eve

uke,

Everything happens for a reason. I'm sorry that you had to endure all of that and after everything that you told me, I can understand why you treated Pilar the way you did. Was it wrong? Yes. You were lashing out at the wrong person. However, at some point, we must talk about forgiveness for what they have done. Not for them, but for you. I'm sure it feels like you have the weight of the world on your shoulders right now, but once you forgive them, a part of that weight will be lifted. Pilar may pretend like she's over it, and she may pretend like she doesn't care, but the Pilar you described to me copes doing other things, correct?

Mandee seems like a nice girl, and I don't think that you should have started dating her when you knew that you were still in love with Pilar. You are hurting people who did nothing wrong because you are hurt. Hurt people, hurt people.

To answer your question, yes, I can still help you. Therapists are very objective.

Thank you for emailing me.

P.S. I really would appreciate it, if you come in and talk to me. I know you said that you wouldn't be able to communicate properly when sitting in front of me, but it can help you learn to communicate better with others.

Sincerely,

Savannah.

I emailed Savannah because I couldn't see myself going into someone's office and talking to them. Plus, I could get my words out better when I texted and shit. I found her email address on her website and was surprised when she emailed me right back. Hopefully, she could help me process some shit.

I was getting ready to go to this New Year's Eve party, but something kept telling me that my babies were going to be born tonight. Pilar's big ass was still holding on to them babies, and we have been going to the damn doctor every day since Christmas. It's like she hasn't moved any. When we came home yesterday, she was only four centimeters.

"Aye, baby mama, you SURE you want me to go out? I mean, you sure your water won't break while I'm out." I stuck my head in the door.

I had been staying here so I could keep a close eye on Pilar because I don't want to miss anything. Plus, I wanted to be around her. Honestly, it's like we are getting to know each other all over again. We were becoming best friends again. Soon, that big nigga is going to be a sweet memory.

"Baby daddy, you can go out. I promise you I am going to call you if I go into labor, okay? I know you tired of being stuck in here with me.

Sorry that my pregnancy is making your schedule crazy," she replied.

"Hey, hey! Don't ever say that again, girl. I'm happy to be here with you."

"I'm happy that you are here. Now, go meet your brothers and my friends at the club. Take a drink or ten for me."

"Alright, fat mama. Call me if you need me," I said. "Pilar, I love you."

She grinned like a little girl. "I love you too. I really do."

When I pulled up to the club, it was jumping. I was in VIP with my brothers. Mandee was there because we had originally planned to bring the New Year in together. You better believe that Swan and Lee were eying her like she had shit on her face. I really couldn't even enjoy myself because I was worried about Pilar being at home alone. Well, she wasn't alone. Mariah was there, but still. I made sure that I had my phone in my shirt pocket so I would be able to hear and feel the vibration in case Pilar called me.

"Duke, can I see your phone? Mine just went dead," Mandee yelled over the music in my ear.

I handed her my phone, and moments later, she placed it back into my pocket. It was five minutes before the countdown to the New Year, and I was pouring drinks getting ready.

"Are we going to fuck tonight?" Mandee whispered seductively in my ear. "I want you to give me those long and deep strokes. My pussy misses you. It's longing for that thick dick."

"I might. If you be a good girl," I said back.

SMACK!

I grabbed my face and looked at a raging Swan.

"PILAR'S WATER BROKE, AND YOU ARE IGNORING HER!" Swan yelled.

"What the fuck are you talking about? She ain't called me. I would have felt the..." I pulled my phone out, pushed the home button, and the screen was blank. "Vibration," I finished my sentence. I powered my phone back on and several messages and voicemails came through.

BITCH, DID YOU TURN MY FUCKING PHONE OFF? IF I WASN'T DONE FUCKING WITH YOU BEFORE, I AM NOW!" I yelled at Mandee.

Swan smacked fire from her ass too, and I was glad that she did because I was getting ready to do it. All of us rushed out of the club and to our cars. I immediately called Mariah back, and all I could hear was Pilar in the background screaming.

"Mariah, put me on speaker, please," I said.

Once she let me know that I was on speaker, I started talking to her.

"Baby, I am on my way. Hold my babies in until I get there. I'm on my way. I'm on my way. I promise. I'm on my way."

"DUKE, SHUT UP AND GET YOUR ASSSSS HEREEEEEE, AHHHH"

I put my emergency lights on and sped to the hospital as quickly and safely as possible. I parked my car in the handicap parking spot and rushed to the hospital. The woman didn't even have to tell me what room she was in, I just followed the screaming voice. I ran into the room and immediately started getting undressed. I grabbed my basketball shorts out of Pilar's bag and put them on. I rushed over and got in the water with her. The nurse was rubbing her back as she was doggy style on the pool.

"Pilar, I'm here, baby. I'm here," I said as I took over rubbing her back.

"Pilar, this first baby is getting ready to come out. You have to find a spot and get as comfortable as you can because once you start pushing you can't move again. Okay?" Dr. Keys said to her, but she didn't say anything.

"Pilar, did you hear Dr. Keys? He said you won't be able to move again."

She nodded her head. Rubbing her back with my left hand and holding her hand with my right, Pilar pushed one big time, and I saw a head pop out.

"Ooowwwee, baby! I see the head! Come on, baby! Give me one more push," I instructed her.

I let her hand go and got behind her. I wanted to pull my own baby out. She pushed one more time, and I caught my baby and immediately put her against my chest.

"Pilar, baby, the girl came out first," I murmured.

The nurse made her cry, and I immediately started crying. It was the best thing I ever heard in my life. She had a head full of curly hair like her mom. Staring down at her, the moment was very indescribable, just like my grandpa said it would be. My heart started racing just holding her against my chest.

"Daddy loves you so much," I cried.

"Come on, Dad! You got one more," Dr. Keys said.

The nurse took her from me and held her while we waited for the boy to come out. Pilar was breathing steady.

"Why you not telling her to push?" I asked Dr. Keys.

"He's not ready yet. Give it another minute or so, and she will be ready to push again," he replied.

I took my baby girl from the nurse and put her in front of Pilar, and she started crying.

"Pilar, look, we made this. This is us, baby!"

"She so beauti...AHHHHH"

"Here he comes," Dr. Keys said.

I handed the nurse back our baby girl, latched on to Pilar's hand, and started rubbing her back. Pilar gave two big pushes, and my baby boy was pushed out into the world. I held him against my chest. The nurse tried to make him cry, but his eyes just opened slowly, and they were the same color as his mom's.

"Wow, he is going to be a tough little cookie. I have rarely seen a baby not cry," Dr. Keys said. "You can get comfortable now."

"Pilar, you did it, baby. You did it!" I placed kisses all over face. "You still look beautiful as shit, girl. I just fell in love with you all over again, damn!"

We stared at them both for like ten minutes straight before the nurses took them away to wash them.

"Hey, after you wash them, put this oil on them. It's from my country, and it's for good luck," I told the nurses.

I couldn't believe that on the first day of the year, God blessed me with a beautiful baby girl and a handsome son. If this was a sign of what my year was going to be like, 2017 was going to be the best year of my life.

PILAR

$\mathcal{D}$ara Merleah Ramses born at 12:15 AM on the first day of the year, and Damel Prince Ramses was born at 12:20 AM. Dara meant beautiful, and Damel meant strong-minded. If I could ever describe perfection, my twins would be it. They both had a head full of curly hair like me, and they both had my eyes. That was pretty much the only thing they got from me. They both had rich chocolate skin like their father. I literally teared up every time I looked at them.

"Baby mama, how could we have made something so perfect," Duke said as he stood over me admiring the twins along with me. "I'm in awe of how cute they are. You know I'm only saying this because they look like me. If they would have looked like you, I would have been mad."

"Hush, I think Damel is going to have a bad attitude, and I am not ready. He hasn't cried yet. I'm worried."

"My mom said I didn't cry much either."

"Duke, do you mind if Ryder comes up? If you say no, I will completely understand, and so will he."

He looked like he had some reservations, but he finally agreed. I texted Ryder and told him to come up. Moments later he walked in with several bags and pink and blue balloons. He set the gifts on the table along with the other gifts and walked over to me.

I took a deep breath and decided to try introducing them again.

"Ryder this is Duke, and Duke this is Ryder."

Reluctantly, Duke grabbed his hand and shook it. The year was starting off good already. Ryder got closer to me, and suddenly, Damel let out the loudest scream ever. Duke immediately took him out my hands, and he calmed down. Duke raised his eyebrow at me, and I squinted at him, letting him know that he better keep it together, because I already knew that he was ready to start some shit.

"Congratulations, baby! Pilar, you look so beautiful. The kids are so beautiful. Duke, thank you for agreeing to let me see her."

Duke nodded his head and kept rocking Damel.

"Well, I have to get back to court. I just wanted to stop in and congratulate you guys. I will talk to you later, okay."

He kissed me on my forehead and walked out my room.

"Melly Mel knows when he is in the presence of a bad spirit. You see he screamed when that nigga got close to you," he said to me and looked down at him. "That's what you do, Mel, protect your mama at all costs."

"First, you will not call our son Melly Mel. Second, he is not a bad guy. Don't do that. I thought you were happy for me."

"I am. I was until Damel told me not to trust that nigga."

I rolled my eyes at his stupid ass. I felt my eyes getting heavy again, but I tried to wait until Swan came back with the food, but my eyelids were winning. Duke took Dara out my arms and told me to get some rest because I was going to need it.

∞

Since I've been home for the past week, I haven't had to do anything, and I mean nothing but sleep and keep my damn milk count up. Who knew that being pregnant was so tiresome. Every time my eyes opened, I was going back to sleep two hours later. While I was sleeping on and off, I was a thousand percent sure that Duke was spoiling the twins. My dad and Karen flew in while my grandparents sent their love.

"Hey, baby, it's time for a feeding. Do you need me to help you to the rocking chair?" Duke barged in the room.

"Duke, I am not handicapped," I assured him.

"Girl, are your breasts hurting? It looks like it, damn! Look like some swollen watermelons."

"Yes, they are, stupid. Come get them started, please."

He got on his knees and got my breasts started. It made it so much easier for the twins to latch.

"Man, just say you want me to suck on your damn titties. If you want daddy to suck on them, then just let me know. You ain't got to be saying shit like 'get my titties started.' You know I'll gladly suck on them juicy thangs. I'll spit the breast milk out, though. That shit is disgusting."

"Shut up, boy, and give me my damn kids.

He handed me the twins, and I latched them on to my breasts.

"Aye, you better make sure Damel is touching his sister. You know how he acts," Duke reminded me.

Since day one, we realized that Damel needed to be touching his damn sister. I swear the only time he cried was when he realized that his sister was no longer near him. We realized that after the first time we fed them separately. I was trying to feed Damel, and he just would not stop hollering. So, we switched them out, and in the midst of us switching babies, they touched, and Damel stopped crying and then started right back. Duke brought it to my attention because he'd noticed a thousand things about them since they've been born. So, Duke handed the other baby to me, and Damel stopped crying again. Of course, Duke had to repeat the action several times, but at least we knew the source of his crying.

After making sure they were latched on good, I scooted Damel over until the top of their heads were touching. They both ate quietly. I looked up, and Duke was staring at me in awe like he always did when I fed them.

"So, what are you doing for your birthday? You going out with your nigga?"

"I want to go to Paris. If he wants to come, he can. My birthday is still kind of far away. You never know what may happen."

"You're right. You never know," he mumbled under his breath and left out the room.

Around the time he and I first started dating, I told him that I wanted to spend my twenty-fifth birthday in Paris. I wondered if he remembered. Well, of course, I wanted to go with him since Paris is the city of love, but things have changed. I also told him that I wouldn't mind getting married in front of the Eiffel Tower. Can you imagine taking a picture of your sparkling ring while the Tower is also sparkling in the back? I didn't even have a dream of getting married until I met Duke, but things change.

After I burped and changed them both, I laid them down on the bed and sat in Indian style in front of them. I played with their little fingers and toes. I never imagined having kids. I never even thought about it, even after all the sex that I was having. Now that they were here, I wouldn't change this feeling for the world. Mel was going to be just like his daddy, and I could tell already.

"Baby mama, are you tired? I can take them."

"No, I'm fine. I just want to look at them."

"Pilar, I am so happy that we are in a good place right now. I couldn't imagine not being able to wake up and go to sleep with them. Thank you for moving in here with me for a little while. Hell, just thank you for pushing out my youngins. When I first caught my daughter… man…the feeling that went through my body…and then my stubborn son…Pilar, I really wanna have like three more, and I only want one baby mama. So, I don't care who you with, baby! When they get about one, I'mma call you up, and be like, 'Aye, it's time for another one.'"

He made me laugh so hard.

"Have they caught Fredrick yet?" I asked.

I was making conversation because I secretly didn't want him to leave. His fresh bath soap made him smell amazing.

"Yeah, they did. He only got multiple charges for Edwina because those other girls didn't want to speak up. He plead not guilty, so he has to go to trial. They kept him in jail with no bond, since she feared for her life."

"Where is she? I know you know."

"Actually, I don't. I'm not worried about her. She's a grown woman, she can take care of herself. Although, I think she stays in the building that my loft is in."

"Hmmmm."

"Don't EVEN start, lil' ugly. You already know where my focus is."

"One more question. What do you think I should do about Demarkus? He ain't bothered me anymore or nothing like that, but I often think about him stalking another girl or placing cameras in their house and shit. I want to tell Robert, but he also got three kids and a wife. If he goes to jail, the kids will suffer."

He held both of his hands on his heart and started wheezing and looking like he was about to have a heart attack. I squinted my eyes at him.

"Oh my God! I am having a heart attack," he said and slid to his knees.

I jumped out the bed and ran to his side.

"Mariiahhh," I yelled, and she instantly ran in the room. "Duke's having a heart attack!"

"I never...never thought I would...see... the day where Pilar Harrison might actually have some sympathy for someone who did her wrong," Duke stuttered out and started laughing.

"BOY!" I yelled and pushed him over. "You had me scared. I should kick your ass."

"Pilar, I'm sorry, but you should have seen your face. Seriously, it's totally up to you what you want to do, but I have to ask…why you feel different?"

"The damn kids, man. The…damn…kids. It's like once you have a baby, EVERYTHING changes— the way you think, the way you feel, the way you look, and all that shit. Damn!"

"I'll tell you what…we will leave him alone for now. Pilar, if he harasses you, or if you even THINK he's following you, then we will go from there. How about that?"

I smiled at him, and he smiled back.

"You don't want me to go, do you?" he asked.

I shook my head. He sat next to me on the bed, and I laid my head on his shoulder as we both stared at the twins while they slept.

RYDER

I had been putting this date off for the last couple of weeks because I already knew what Pilar wanted to do. She wanted to stop dating me. I knew it. I could feel it in my bones. I should have known that once those kids came, she would think she was still in love with their father. I really liked her. Pilar was cool as fuck and funny. I knew that she was still harboring some type of feelings for that nigga because she hardly ever wanted to talk about why they broke up.

Niggas would probably look at me stupid because I was cool with her living in the house with her ex, but she made me secure because I would randomly FaceTime her, and she would answer. She could be sitting next to him while talking to me and nothing would change, so I was very secure. I grabbed my briefcase and locked up my office. I drove as slow as I could to the restaurant where Pilar was waiting for me.

As soon as I stepped in, Pilar waved me over. She stood up to hug me, and she looked good to have had two babies not long ago. I took my seat, and I could feel my heart start to speed up.

"Ryder, the reason I called you here is because we have to stop dating. It's seriously not about Duke or anyone else. I just realized that I needed time to myself. I didn't take the time for myself after my horrible break up with Duke, and it was not fair to you. I'm sorry. I hope you don't hate me."

I sighed deeply before replying, "I don't hate you, and I completely understand where you are coming from. I hope that we can still be friends, and maybe one day, we can jump back in this dating thing. You are one of a kind."

"I know, baby! Well, I must get going. I don't mean to cut dinner short, but I just didn't want to tell you this over the phone."

She got up, gave me a hug, and walked out of the restaurant. Since it was still kind of early, I could go back to my office and get just a little more work done since I wouldn't be rushing home to talk to her.

"I thought I told you to leave her alone."

I looked up and saw Demarkus at the door.

"You're a stalker now? Why am I not surprised? You always did weird shit like this when girls didn't want your ass. You need to move on. Didn't your *wife* have a baby not long ago or some shit?"

I could have easily told him that Pilar broke it off with me, but his ass ain't need to know shit. Fuck him.

"Fuck you!" he snapped.

He pulled his gun on me and cocked it. My hands went up. This nigga had a crazy look in his eyes, and I wasn't sure if this nigga was going to shoot me or not.

"Look, Demarkus...."

"Oh now, it's '*Look, Demarkus*?' Where is all that smart shit now?

Fuck you. I'll see your ass in hell."

Demarkus let off three shots into my chest, and I covered my chest trying to stop the blood from oozing out. I began to cough up blood, and he stood there watching me. The last thought that I had was that he better not touch a hair on Pilar's head.

PILAR

$\mathcal{D}$uke and I had just made it home from the twins' first check-up. Dr. Keys said that they were doing just fine and were some healthy babies. I'm still adjusting to being a mom, but I was getting the hang of it. I really salute women who make this shit look like a piece of cake because it is not. I swear to God the first time that Dara had an explosive shit, I wanted to stamp her little ass with a return to sender stamp. I did not sign up to be cleaning up explosive shit. She lit up the whole front room. Duke laughed hard at me as I struggled with not trying to throw her away.

I had just laid them both down for a nap when there was a loud ass knock on the door. I was heading to the door when Duke stopped me, moved me behind him, and he answered the door.

"Is Pilar Harrison here?"

"What can I help you with?"

"We came to talk to Pilar."

"You *came* to my doorstep. So, I have the right to know what you need with the mother of my children. You ain't even introduce yourself."

"The security guard had to call you for you to let us in, so you know our names."

To keep Duke out of jail, I moved from behind the door, and it was detectives Cliff and Sam. I rolled my eyes because they were here on some bullshit about that Brandon case. Seriously?

"There she is. What kind of pussy do you have that every nigga you fuck with comes up dead?" Cliff smirked.

Duke tried to rush him, but he pulled his gun out on him. I pushed Duke back.

"What are you talking about? The last man I gave my pussy to is right here getting ready to beat the brakes off you."

"So, maybe this is who would want Ryder Sandford dead. You were seen with him yesterday."

I instantly slammed the door to get myself together. Ryder was dead. I looked up at Duke, and he looked down at me.

"Please, tell me that you didn't," I whispered.

"Pilar, you ain't even got to ask me that. I have been here with your tack head ass all day, every day since my kids been born. You better check with one of your other niggas," he spat.

It was like a light bulb went off in my head. I knew who did it, but would the police believe me?

"Duke, give me that camera and shit. I'm going with them to the station. I'll be right back."

"Pilar, I ain't letting you go with them niggas by yourself. I will drive you there myself. Let me call Baron and Swan to come down here right quick. Since Mariah has the day off, I don't want to bother her."

"Okay."

I opened the door back and told him that we would follow him to the station in a minute and that they both can wait outside. Ten minutes later, Swan and Baron pulled up on the golf cart. Duke and I got in his car and was following them to the station.

"This is ridiculous. Why the fuck would he kill Ryder?" I said to myself.

"Pilar, I'mma ask you something, and I want you to be honest with me."

My heart started beating fast because I knew what he was about to ask me. I nodded my head.

"Did you fuck Demarkus?"

"Yeah. I did," I whispered.

I noticed his fingers started to clench harder around the steering wheel. I didn't want to say anything because I knew he was pissed.

"I'm pissed, Pilar! I'm real pissed, but it's all good. That's why he killed that nigga; you put that pussy on him. You got that killer pussy. I'll body a nigga over that pussy too."

"Shut up, Duke."

We pulled up to the police station and walked inside. They told Duke to wait because they only wanted to speak to me. I noticed Robert and Demarkus in his office talking. He looked at me and winked. I wanted to vomit.

Back in the cold room, Cliff and Sam were glaring at me, and I was glaring at them back.

"I guess we could call you black widow, huh?" Cliff said.

"Call me what you want, but I'm not involved in this no type of way. Yes, we went out to dinner, and I was only there to break it off with him. After that, I don't know where he went. My kids' father was home with me. I know who did it, though, and this time I am proud to snitch because he is a creep. I was going to spare him, but nah, not anymore. Can you please call Robert and Demarkus in here?" I spoke.

They entered the room moments later.

"Um, I believe this belongs to y'all," I said and pulled the small camera out of my pocket. I placed it on the table, and they all looked crazy in the face.

"In Demarkus's spare time, he likes to watch me have sex with the father of my children. He is also a stalker, and I just know that it is probably him behind this."

"You lying bitch," Demarkus snapped.

Robert grabbed his arm, did some type of move on his ass, and slammed his face against the table.

"Don't you ever disrespect my granddaughter again. You did leave for hours yesterday. Where did you go? You already in trouble for stealing property from here and illegally setting it up in someone's house. I'mma ask you again, where…were…you…yesterday?"

"Cap, I know you are not going⊠"

Robert pushed his face harder into the table.

"One last time."

"I WANT MY LAWYER!" Demarkus yelled like a bitch.

"Well, it looks like my services are no longer needed here," I said before I got up and left out the room.

I met Duke back in the lobby, and he stood up to greet me.

"What happened?" he asked.

"I think Demarkus is about to sing like a canary. Let's go home to our kids."

"The only place I wanna be."

We smiled at each other, and I saw the person that I fell in love with.

PILAR

Birthday

$\mathcal{H}$ere I was sitting on a bench in front of the Eiffel Tower five minutes before I turned twenty-five. Duke even bought me the ticket for my birthday. He was pissed that I was going by myself, but I insisted that I would be fine. I was only going to be here today and tomorrow because I wanted to get back to the twins. Reflecting on this past year of my life had me in my feelings so bad. This past year, I had so many ups and downs, but overall, I found myself. Duke and I are co-parenting better than I thought we would. We still lived together. I'm not sure if he was dating or not because he was gone a lot more now. My relationships with my family were intact. I didn't know if Lenora or Cisco would be proud, especially since I found out that Lenora kept Prince away from me on purpose. Duke was able to get me that box that I got from her house a long time ago. It was full of letters addressed from Prince to me, the letters between Prince and 'his Coco,' and a whole bunch of checks. Of course, it was too late to cash them, but I decided to keep them. Their love was wrong, but it was sweet. Just from the letters, I knew that he loved her very much.

Lenora wrote a letter, and it was the last letter in the box. She said that she kept me away from him on purpose because of his life in the streets that he thought no one knew about. She said that she didn't want to use his drug money to take care of me, which I didn't get because she would let old ass men jack off to me and take their money. She had to have been drunk while writing it. She told me that she never approved of their relationship to begin with and believes that he was the reason that she was dead. After that, I balled the letter up and threw it away. I didn't want to have any more negative thoughts about her.

On the news, I saw that they had finally sentenced Fredrick's ass to fifty years in prison, and Demarkus would spend the rest of his life in jail for the murder of Ryder. Savannah told me that I didn't need to blame myself for Demarkus's mess, but it was hard not to. Robert and I's relationship was still strained because of his wife, so I didn't see him much, but he still called and checks on the twins. He also sends me toys and stuff for them.

I was looking at my watch counting down the seconds until I turned twenty-five. Five…four…three…two…one.

"Did you think I was going to let you celebrate an important milestone in your life in a different country by yourself?" I looked up, and saw Duke leaning on the back on the bench.

"Duke, what are you doing here?" I asked.

"When I first met this beautiful, mean girl who always called me a 'fuck-boy,' I knew that I wanted to fuck. Hell, I knew I was going to fuck, but what I didn't know… I didn't know that I was going to fall so deep in love with her," he said before he sat next to me.

I turned to face him. He grabbed my hands.

"Pilar, I wish there was something I could do to make up for all the bad shit that I did and said to you. Instead of asking how I could help or what did you need me to do, I flaked on you. When you needed me the most, I cowered out. I'm sorry for leaving you to go through most of the pregnancy alone. I missed the first kicks and the first hiccups, but I promise I won't miss shit else. Pilar, I am truly sorry for lying to you about my life back in Egypt, but I didn't want to lose you. I couldn't lose you. I know I acted like I ain't give a fuck, but the whole time, I could barely sleep and barely eat. I was using other people to take my mind off you, but that shit ain't work. My heart beats for your lil' cat-eyed, curly haired ass."

The tears started streaming down my face because Duke finally apologized and meant it from a place that I knew was sincere. The look in his eyes told me that he was serious. We stared at each other for a moment. Suddenly, I heard violins start playing one of my favorite songs, "Always and Forever" by Luther Vandross. Duke slowly got on one knee in front of me, slid my leather glove off, and held my hand as the violinists played. People were stopping and starting to record. I was getting nervous. The only thing that was going through my head was Savannah's words, *When the time comes, and you choose Duke, because you WILL choose him...* She was right. I was choosing him. It was always going to be him.

"I remember when you told me about Paris being the city of love. You ain't tell me it was the city of cold either. My nuts about to freeze off," he laughed. "Seriously, months ago, when I asked you what type of proposal you wanted, you told me that you would love to get proposed to in the city of love. I always had that in the back of mind because I knew the moment our lips touched, we were meant to be together. I knew that you were going to be my wife. When you pushed out my children, that made me love you even more. Honestly, I can't imagine life without you, and please, don't make me. You got my mind, my soul, and most importantly my heart, and I don't ever want you to give it back. So, I got one question to ask you. Can I be the only one to fuck you for the rest of your life? I'm playing...not really. Will you make me the happiest man in the whole world and marry me?

"Yes, Duke, yes! I choose you! It was always you. It will always be you!"

He slid the ring on my finger. At first, I thought it was going to be the ring that he proposed to me with at first, but it wasn't. This ring was bigger and perfect. We shared one long passionate kiss, and there was a lot of screaming and shouting around us. I looked up, and we had drawn a crowd of people.

He grabbed my hand and led me to two people— a much older version of himself and a beautiful woman.

"Pilar, these are the two most important people in my life, my grandma and grandpa. I honestly can't wait to marry you. So, my grandpa is going to marry us right here and right now."

"Duke, are you serious? Wait. Where are the twins? What about your crown? What about your country's law?" I shot off question after question.

I was so nervous. I wanted to marry him, but I didn't know he wanted to marry me like right now.

"Shhh. You are thinking too much. My crown didn't come with you, so I didn't want it. Everything will be taken care of, and that is all that matters," he said.

"Well, I guess I will, especially after looking at what you are going to age into. Sheesh. You are going to be one hot old man." I laughed.

Duke's grandpa winked at me.

He took my hands in his, and his grandpa started the ceremony. This is how I always pictured my wedding— very intimate with the person I love, and then we throw a big party afterwards. Duke and I said our vows and sealed our marriage with a kiss.

"YASSSSS, BITCH, YASSSS," I looked over and saw Swan yelling.

She was accompanied by Baron, Lee, Bomani, Savannah, Dr. Keys, Prince, and Karen, the people that changed my life for the better. I looked up and little flakes of snow started to fall on top of us.

"How long have you been working on this? How did you get them to come?" I asked.

"Well, when you said you wanted to go to Paris for your birthday, I already knew what was going to happen. I bought all our tickets the same day," he replied. "I know you said you wanted a ceremony with just us, so I told them not to make any noise until after you said, 'I Do.'"

This man was something else, and he really made me happy.

"Mrs. Ramses, can we go inside so my balls can thaw out?" Duke said.

"Yes, Mr. Ramses. Yes, we can."

We walked hand in hand over to our crowd of friends, and family. This had to be one of the best days of my life. I never imagined I would leave Paris a married woman. It was a day that I would never forget.

EPILOGUE: DUKE

1 year later

$\mathcal{M}$arrying Pilar had to be the best decision that I ever made in my life. Since we've been married, the sex had been better, and we have been better to each other. We both still see Savannah, and she makes our life better. There is nothing going wrong with our marriage, but a once a month check-up doesn't hurt to make sure things continue to go great.

As far as Dutch's ass, Savannah told me that the more I tortured him, the more I hung on to the hurt that he caused myself and my wife. So, after I told my grandpa that I was finally letting go, he took him out to the ocean, where he tied him to an anchor, threw him overboard, and let my father drown. I knew it hurt my grandpa to kill his last son, but he said he would cope with it the best way he knew how. Once the crowd got wind of Dutch's death, it was like they rejoiced more than mourned.

Pilar forgave Bakari, but she said she didn't want to talk to him anymore, and that is alright with me. We recently just hugged, and that was at my niece's birthday party. Pilar didn't attend, but I did bring the twins. Since I forfeited my crown, and neither Baron nor Bomani qualified for the position because of their relations with American women, Bakari was left. He got the position he wanted, and honestly, he was damn good at it. He loved the attention. My moms didn't really accept Pilar as my wife at first, but like I told them, it was either both of us or none of us. They fell right in line. I didn't give a damn about what the people in my country thought, so I honestly didn't know how they felt about me marrying the love of my life.

"Daddy, can you please tie my shoes. I can't see my feet. I swear, I'm going to stop fucking you," Pilar waddled in the room.

She was seven months pregnant with another daughter, and I was so excited.

"Who I look like?"

"The nigga that's gon' tie my shoes. Where the twins? Why do I hear them yelling? Do you not have them ready? Duke, we are going to be late. Oh my God!"

"First, calm down, mama! We are going to be on time. It doesn't even open for another two hours. Don't get your nerves worked up. Everything is going to turn out fine."

Pilar had been working tirelessly to open her own non-profit organization for women, including rape survivors, battered women, and endangered youth. I was so proud of her when she finally got approved from the state and received several grants. I could have given her the money, but she said that this is something that she wanted to do on her own to put her degree to use. She even hired Edwina as a youth counselor. She figured that the young girls could learn from her since she claimed to have turned her life around. She was not allowed to talk to me at all. Her organization was called P's Peace. According to how this one went, she would open another one in another state, but for now, we are going to start in Jacksonville.

"I'm so nervous. What if it doesn't work out?" she said.

"What if it does? Stop worrying, girl."

I yelled out something in Arabic to the twins, and they came and stood front and center. I play with them a lot, but when my voice goes up an octave, they stop doing whatever they are doing.

"What I tell you about speaking that around me? You know I still don't know that shit…I mean that stuff…that language," Pilar said.

"Well, whenever I try to teach you, you get mad and frustrated. So, what am I to do?" I replied.

"We ain't got time to talk about that right now. Let's go," she snapped.

I looked at her with a confused look on my face because she started the conversation, and then got mad, and wanted to end the conversation. I chuckled at her as I grabbed the bags, and we all headed for the door. When I finished locking the house up, I turned and looked at my family walking to the truck.

It's funny how life works. The one person that I couldn't stand at all was now my wife. We went through a lot of shit, and I do mean a lot of shit, but if I had to do it all over again and this be the outcome, then I would in a heartbeat. Her heart was worth much more than my crown on any day.

THE END

MESSAGE FROM AUTHORESS BIANCA

Hey, y'all! Thank you all so much for the love and constant support. When you get finished reading, please let me know how much you loved this book, with a review. It really means so much. As always, I have to thank God for blessing me with this talent that I never knew I had. I have to thank my, P. Mae Sterling, for giving my talent the vision back in January of 2016. My Royalty sisters, I love you all so much for being such a constant support and being such a strong group of women. Last, but certainly not least, I have to thank my readers. You guys give me the strength I need to continue to write. Reading your reviews and inbox messages make me feel so loved. Thank you for taking a chance on this new author.

With Love,

Bianca

CONNECT WITH ME ON SOCIAL MEDIA:

Facebook Readers Group: www.facebook.com/groups/AuthoressBianca/

Facebook Like Page: www.facebook.com/AuthoressBianca

Instagram: @AuthoressBianca

OTHER NOVELS BY BIANCA

www.amazon.com/author/bianca

Subscribe to my website: www.authoressbianca.com

Looking for a publishing home?

Royalty Publishing House, Where the Royals reside, is accepting submissions for writers in the urban fiction genre. If you're interested, submit the first 3-4 chapters with your synopsis to submissions@royaltypublishinghouse.com.

Check out our website for more information: www.royaltypublishinghouse.com.

Text ROYALTY to 42828 to join our mailing list!
To submit a manuscript for our review, email us at
submissions@royaltypublishinghouse.com

Text RPHCHRISTIAN to 22828 for our
CHRISTIAN ROMANCE novels!

Text RPHROMANCE to 22828 for our
INTERRACIAL ROMANCE novels!

Get LiT!

Download the LiT eReader app today and enjoy exclusive content, free books, and more

Get These Exclusively on LiT

Do You Like CELEBRITY GOSSIP?

Check Out QUEEN DYNASTY!
Visit Our Site: www.thequeendynasty.com

11788896R00144

Made in the USA
Lexington, KY
15 October 2018